THE NIGHT STALKER RESCUE

A SHADOW STRIKE NOVELLA

JASON KASPER

SEVERN RIVER
PUBLISHING

Severn River Publishing
SevernRiverBooks.com

This is a work of fiction. Names, characters, businesses, places, events and incidents are either the products of the author's imagination or used in a fictitious manner. Any resemblance to actual persons, living or dead, or actual events is purely coincidental.

ISBN: 978-1-64875-060-1 (Paperback)

ALSO BY JASON KASPER

American Mercenary Series
Greatest Enemy
Offer of Revenge
Dark Redemption
Vengeance Calling
The Suicide Cartel
Terminal Objective

Shadow Strike Series
The Enemies of My Country
Last Target Standing
Covert Kill
Narco Assassins
Beast Three Six

Spider Heist Thrillers
The Spider Heist
The Sky Thieves
The Manhattan Job
The Fifth Bandit

Standalone Thriller
Her Dark Silence

To find out more about Jason Kasper and his books, visit
severnriverbooks.com/authors/jason-kasper

THE NIGHT STALKER RESCUE

Jolo Island, Philippines

The jungle blazed in my night vision, a luminescent universe of bright green extending up the steep volcanic slope.

Clambering up the thickly jungled hillside was loud, but stealth wasn't an issue—not yet. A chattering chorus of insects and amphibians concealed our movement, and I felt reasonably confident that no bad guys were out here at this time of night, clinging to the slope. They didn't have to be. After all, the Abu Sayyaf Group owned a significant portion of this island, moving freely among their jungle bases and enjoying the support of a local populace with abundant familial ties.

But we couldn't take any chances under the best of circumstances, and it didn't help that our intelligence couldn't tell us whether to expect twenty bad guys along our route, or a hundred.

I glanced to my right and left, verifying that a teammate still trailed me on either side. They were visible only in fleeting glimpses through a labyrinth of vegetation, appearing as shadowy silhouettes that moved as I did: suppressed rifles at the ready, faces half-covered by night vision devices.

Together, our three-man wedge formation followed the point man as he threaded his way uphill.

My team had packed light for our inaugural mission, wearing assault packs with just enough water and supplies for a two-night operation. But weight was relative in this hazardous terrain, particularly when we'd all sweated through our fatigues within minutes of entering the sweltering jungle.

We carried HK416s, gas piston rifles that fired the same 5.56mm round widely used by the island's many jihadist terrorists. Sure, our guns had a few key differences from your average outdated insurgent weapon—optics, infrared lasers, suppressors, and subsonic ammo—but none of that would matter once we were gone. When we left this island in two days' time, the only evidence of American passing would be bootprints, expended shell casings, and, if all went according to plan, one dead terrorist leader.

My radio earpiece crackled with a genteel Southern accent —Worthy, our point man.

"I can see the crest, David. We're almost there."

I breathed a sigh of relief in the humid night air and transmitted back in a whisper.

"Copy, let's take a short halt at the top."

As I advanced a few meters up the slope toward the crest, the dense wall of foliage gave way to clear sky. By the time I reached the top, I faced a breathtaking view.

The short scrub brush and scattered trees of the high ground fell away to reveal Jolo Island's interior, a rippling expanse of jungle and crop fields, a round crater lake, and a jagged coastline ending at a flat, calm sea. A brilliant galaxy of stars glittered overhead, and I scarcely had time to observe the sight before a breeze washed over my sweat-soaked face. The cool night air, salty with seawater, was a welcome respite from the humidity and swarms of mosquitoes we'd fought through to get here. Now that we'd arrived at the high ground, we could easily follow this volcanic ridge to reach our bed-down site well before sunrise.

I approached Worthy, now on a knee and pulling front security. He had the least operational experience of any of us, and that made him a liability. But a childhood spent in the forests and swamps of south Georgia with his hunting guide father had endowed him with a preternatural ability to navigate through the most heinous terrain with ease and, perhaps more importantly, detect the slightest thing out of place with the natural surroundings.

He was eager to prove himself, and I'd made the decision to employ him as the team point man. This mission would tell if I'd chosen wisely or not, and I hoped that uncertainty accounted for the light quivering in my stomach, growing in intensity and hinting that something was about to go terribly wrong.

I stopped behind Worthy's kneeling figure, taking a knee to face back the way we'd come, and watched as our remaining two teammates climbed onto the ridge, approaching like a pair of green ghosts in my night vision.

It was easy enough to tell who was who—apart from my familiarity with operating alongside them at night, they couldn't have been more different.

Reilly, our medic, possessed a heart as big as his torso. His broad shoulders made the rifle in his grasp seem like a plaything as he took a knee to my right, picking up a sector of fire and whispering in his boyish voice, a near-lisp marking the last word.

"Well, that sucked."

Our fourth man closed in, his lanky frame moving at a casual saunter. His real name was Alan, but everyone called him Cancer. I'd first named him that because of his affinity for cigarettes, though he claimed it was because he'd killed more men than cancer. While he was a highly trained sniper, tonight he carried a suppressed HK416 in anticipation of shooting up close and personal.

Cancer knelt beside me, completing our tight 360 perimeter and addressing the point man in his raspy Jersey lilt.

"Find enough thorn patches to walk us through, asshole?"

Trading his unflappably polished Southern accent for a crude Austrian one, Worthy calmly replied, "What's the matter? The CIA got you pushing too many pencils?"

I shook my head mournfully.

During a break in training last week, we'd watched the '80s Schwarzenegger classic Predator in our team room. Cancer had made a halfhearted comment that whoever had the best use of a movie quote on this Philippines mission should get a case of beer, paid for by his teammates—and this casual remark had ignited a firestorm of Predator references, from the remainder of our planning up until we'd slipped into the jungle hours ago.

"Let's pick it up," I said. "Catch our breath on an easy descent, and—"

Then Reilly hissed one word that stopped me in my tracks.

"Helicopter!"

We leapt to our feet in a flash, scattering away from one another as each man sought the cover of trees in the clearing.

I threw my back against a tree trunk, peeking out and trying to catch sight of the aircraft. Before I could locate it, Reilly transmitted over my earpiece.

"David, I've got eyes on—it's headed right for us. Ten seconds out."

I swallowed hard, feeling the hair lift on the back of my neck. The rhythmic throbbing of insect calls continued, quieter here on the ridge—but even with the jungle noise, we should have had more than ten seconds' notice from any approaching helicopter.

How had it managed to sneak up on us?

I got my answer a second later when Cancer transmitted,

"That's a Little Bird."

The second I heard it, I knew he was right. The approaching rotor noise was unmistakable—a thin buzzing whir almost comically quiet compared to other helicopters in the US arsenal. The Little Bird was so named for good reason: it was absurdly small, requiring the two pilots to sit nearly shoulder to shoulder.

But small didn't mean it wasn't deadly.

Little Birds were outfitted in one of two configurations: either with armament for attack purposes or benches to deposit groups of highly trained assaulters. Either was a terrorist's worst nightmare and, regrettably at present, equally nightmarish to my team.

Because the two American pilots screaming toward our position were mere seconds away, and on their thermal display we'd be indistinguishable from the violent extremists swarming across this island.

And while indiscriminate strikes were not the hallmark of US military pilots, the fact remained that none of them knew my team was here. We'd programmed a multitude of American and Philippine military frequencies in our radios but were expressly forbidden from making contact. Due to the nature of our mission, we lacked any legal protection afforded a sanctioned unit. That much was by design, though I now feared this safeguard was about to get us killed an hour into our first mission.

My heart hammered in my throat as the buzz of rotor blades grew in volume until it was nearly on top of us; in seconds, we'd know if the pilots would ignore us or perceive us as a threat.

But the helicopter's noise peaked a moment before it reached us, then faded. I looked out from behind my tree as the tiny helicopter banked away from our position. Under night vision it looked like little more than a dark egg with rotors, and I saw at once that my fears of being shot at were unfounded. This aircraft wasn't configured for attack but troop insertion—and the exterior benches were bare, a neat square of night sky momentarily visible through the empty fuselage. Whatever their mission, the two pilots were headed back to their staging area, likely one of the Navy amphibious assault ships currently operating off the island's north coast.

As the helicopter soared toward the sea, I transmitted, "All right, let's pick it back up and—"

But I never got to finish.

The words died on my lips as a cluster of explosions sounded in the distance, a terrifying cacophony of booms followed by the hiss of rockets.

I swung my night vision device toward the departing helicopter, locating it in the distance just in time to register a flash of light.

The sound of the explosion reached me a half-second later, and the spark of flame darkened to reveal the Little Bird spinning wildly before disappearing into the jungle beneath a smoky pyramid of rockets that streaked skyward, victorious.

My stomach turned to stone, my momentary disbelief vanishing as I shouted, "Worthy, take us there!"

The only confirmation that he'd heard me came as he appeared in the clearing, running toward the far slope.

Cancer, Reilly, and I followed suit, wordlessly falling into a tight single file—not the most tactically sound formation, but by far and away the fastest. If there was any time to sacrifice security for speed, this was it.

Together the four of us crashed downhill, abandoning any attempt at noise discipline.

We moved as quickly as the vegetation would allow, each man struggling to keep the teammate to his front in sight through the leaves. We needed no discussion about our next actions—an American helo was down, and the enemy would be swarming over the crash site as fast as they could reach it. If my team didn't make it there first, the pilots would fall into the hands of a terrorist enemy whose calling card was decapitation.

I keyed a button to transmit over the command frequency, speaking breathlessly as I ran.

"Angel One, Angel One," I gasped. "These fuckers just took down a Little Bird. We're hauling ass to the crash site."

No return transmission came over my earpiece, and I was about to repeat the call when I heard a response: the nasal voice of an extremely calm man referencing me by callsign.

"Suicide, this is Angel One. Copy all. I'm on it."

I gave no thought to what "it" meant for Ian, whose callsign of Angel One had been well-earned. In the intelligence world, Ian was a miracle worker; his expert analysis and boundless intellect were almost without peer. But his options now were limited—Ian was currently loitering offshore in the fishing vessel that had inserted my team on the beach, his only weapon at present a communications suite that served as the sole link to our higher command.

I directed my thoughts to the tactical situation.

This attack was no chance encounter. The odds of an RPG hitting, much less downing, a helicopter were absurdly small. So the implications of a coordinated RPG salvo were clear—this ambush was a well-planned and executed operation to capture US pilots.

And on this part of the island, that meant one man was responsible.

We'd been sent to kill him, the attack planned for tomorrow night, but our orders had apparently come one night too late. Now we were reacting to his plan, racing against a savage force of enemy fighters to recover two pilots whether they were living or dead.

Ahead of me, Worthy abruptly halted his downhill movement.

I stopped too, assuming he just needed a moment to evaluate his choice of path through the jungle's myriad obstacles.

But instead of continuing movement, he transmitted a radio call.

"David, I can make out a campfire ahead—two, maybe three guys. We can probably redirect around them to bypass."

"Negative," I transmitted, "we're going to hit them and go straight through. I'll initiate. Get on line."

Reilly and Cancer needed no encouragement from me; as Worthy held his fixed position, the three of us advanced on either side of him to form a consolidated front. No civilians inhabited this part of the island, and by the time we swung wide to bypass the campfire, we'd lose time we didn't have to spare. I likewise had no interest in leaving an enemy element alive to our rear, where we'd be most vulnerable to tracking and pursuit.

Besides, I thought, we were already uphill of the campfire. In a gunfight, occupying an elevated position against your opponent was practically half the battle.

We advanced down the slope, remaining on line with one another. The campfire's glow was now visible to each of us, and after we'd advanced slightly, so were the men around it.

They were dancing, laughing, and hoisting their rifles like they'd just scored the winning goal at the World Cup. For an organization like Abu Sayyaf, downing an American military chopper was a far greater achievement, and these three men appeared to be celebrating the victory with glee. Their silhouettes were green shadows flitting in the center of their camp, our infrared lasers flickering in and out of visibility against the glowing blaze of the fire.

I could only make out the three men through the leaves, and tried to hold my fire until the last possible moment as we crept closer. If any additional forces were present, the element of surprise wouldn't count for much, and we needed to kill as many as possible in the opening salvo to have any chance of wiping them out completely.

But I saw no one else, and we were now only a few meters distant. If we got much closer, the fire would glint off the lens of a night vision device, alerting them that they were no longer alone.

When my next footfall landed on the damp bed of leaf litter, I stopped in place. Flicking my rifle's selector lever from safe to semiautomatic, I opened fire on the center man.

My subsonic bullet found its mark, causing the man to jolt violently as I chased the first shot with three more, then swung my barrel left.

I heard the hissing plinks of four suppressed rifles shooting in unison. My aim found the next man, who was already being drilled with bullets. I got two shots off before he fell, and by the time I searched for the third man, he'd already dropped out of sight.

I called out, "Advance!"

We moved forward on line, taking deliberate steps in a measured approach. My senses were on hyperalert, waiting for return fire to ring out, for unseen enemies to open fire from our flanks.

But the rhythmic symphony of night creatures continued unabated around us. Creeping toward the edge of the trees, we found the three fallen bodies motionless around the small campfire. We fired another volley of suppressed gunfire, achieving stationary headshots that ejected splatters of brain matter across the jungle floor.

Then we crossed through the small encampment, spreading ourselves wide around the fire as we swept our barrels across ponchos and tarps strung up as outpost shelters. But I saw no other enemy, no survivors rallying in a counterattack to our intrusion.

"You guys got anything?" I called out.

A trio of responses in the negative.

I glanced back toward the small outpost we'd just cleared.

There was no time to search the bodies and likely no intelligence to recover if we did, but my view fell on a small handheld radio propped against a log. I darted to grab it and then turned it off immediately—the last thing I needed was to have our position compromised by an errant enemy transmission. After stuffing the radio in my cargo pocket, I called out, "Worthy, let's go."

The action was over as quickly as it had begun, and then we were off again, reloading on the move as we followed Worthy downhill in a single file. Disadvantaged from the start, my team was running out of time; the enemy had surely staged forces to pounce on a downed chopper, and, short of a miracle, they'd be at the crash site long before we would. Our only advantage was that no one knew we were here, and we'd have to approach the crash site like we had the small enemy outpost—come in hot, using speed and surprise to compensate for our lack of numbers. After the initial shots, everything that followed would be an instinctive play-by-play, with us reacting to chaos as it unfolded in a desperate bid to save the pilots before they fell victim to a far worse fate.

Ian's voice came over the command frequency.

"Suicide, this is Angel One. Cease movement to crash site, I say again cease movement now."

"Negative," I replied, not breaking stride. "You out of your fucking mind?"

"Listen to me. Radio chatter indicates forty enemy fighters there."

"Well, in a few minutes there's going to be zero enemy fighters there."

"They're calling for reinforcements and splitting into search parties. They only recovered one dead pilot."

I felt a wave of lightheadedness, as if suddenly overcome with vertigo. I couldn't have heard him correctly.

"Say again," I said curtly.

"There was only one pilot in the wreckage. He was dead when they got there. Whoever flew that bird with him is evading in the jungle. You've got a survivor to find."

I momentarily released my grip on the transmit switch, my mind going delirious with relief. How was this possible? In this preplanned attack, the enemy would have been swarming the crash site within minutes. With forty fighters charging the wreck, how had the surviving pilot possibly slipped into the jungle before being captured?

Ian continued, "My assessment is that this pilot will be headed due north. The US amphibious fleet is already dispatching boats to the coast. By the time the pilot gets there, he'll have Navy vessels patrolling to find him."

We had to change course fast—we were still moving at a brisk clip, though the increased density of plant life slowed our descent toward the low ground. Before I could confirm that my team had heard Ian's transmission, Worthy was already redirecting our movement and transmitting, "Shifting course northwest."

I quickly resumed communications with Ian over the command net.

"Did we load a frequency for his survival radio?" It was a valid question—Ian had loaded so many contingency frequencies into our radios that I couldn't keep them straight short of consulting the coded list I carried, and there was no time for that now.

"Channel 32 on your command radio is the emergency frequency. If the pilot took his survival radio out of that wreck, that's what he'll be tuned into. I already transmitted that your team is inbound. No response from the pilot, but that could be because I'm outside of range."

Or because he was too busy running for his life to answer.

"Callsign?"

"Aircraft callsign was Beast Three Six."

I flipped the channel of my command radio to the survival frequency—no small feat when moving through the jungle at night—and transmitted at once.

"Beast Three Six, Beast Three Six. This is an American ground unit approximately one klick northwest of your crash site. We are moving north to link up along your evasion route to the north. Send your location when able."

I continued moving, the prospect of a response dancing like butterflies in my stomach. But I heard nothing, which, I supposed, was to be expected. For the pilot, activating much less monitoring his radio wouldn't be a priority while he could hear the enemy combing the jungle to find him. The onus was on me to make radio contact, and I'd have to repeat the message every few minutes until he replied.

In the meantime, I marveled at the fact that a survivor had managed to slip away from the wreckage. Whoever this pilot was, now on the run in a desperate attempt to evade capture, I knew only one thing for certain: he was very, very good.

That much shouldn't have come as a surprise.

The enemy had shot down a Little Bird, and those were flown by the Army's 160th SOAR—Special Operations Aviation Regiment. To call that organization legendary would be an offense to their true accomplishments worldwide, most of which were highly classified. Simply put, the 160th flew the most high-risk missions imaginable, using the most specialized helicopters on the planet, with a unit creed proclaiming their ability to arrive on target plus or minus thirty seconds anywhere in the world.

But like every storied military unit throughout history, the true strength of the 160th lay not in their equipment, but their people.

Our surviving pilot was a Night Stalker, the 160th's not-so-unofficial nickname, and that term carried a lot of hard-earned implications. Night Stalker crews underwent extensive training in evading capture, so we were dealing with a pro. He'd already managed to flee the wreckage, which was impressive enough—now, his priority would be to distance himself from the crash site and stay hidden until the first search and rescue team arrived.

Given our chance proximity to an aircraft shootdown on this island, that first team would be us.

I tried contacting him again. Still no response.

I consulted my GPS as we moved. The accuracy was degraded when under thick canopy, but we would be intersecting the azimuth due north of the crash site soon. However, until we received a response from the pilot, we could do little but follow his likely path toward the coast, transmitting every few minutes while trying to duck enemy patrols.

But the sun would be rising soon, raising the stakes for everyone.

I sent a third radio transmission.

"Beast Three Six, American ground unit now approximately five hundred meters north of the crash site. Send your location."

No response.

Irritated, I let go of my transmit switch and searched for Worthy's form moving through the leaves ahead.

He was gone.

I stopped for a moment, looking left and right and realizing that I should have been able to see him.

Then I heard repeated bursts of static over my earpiece—he was keying his radio repeatedly, signaling that he was unable to verbally transmit.

I threw myself to the jungle floor, knowing that Cancer and Reilly would do the same behind me. Readying my weapon from the prone, I tried to sense whatever Worthy had detected —he'd chosen to "go to ground" rather than open fire, so he must have sensed at least a chance of us evading enemy contact.

Trying to slow my breathing, I listened to the night jungle

humming around me. I detected nothing out of place, so Worthy's cue must have been visual—and from ground level, my nostrils thick with the smell of rotting leaf litter and mud, I could see nothing.

As it turned out, I didn't have to.

Instead, I heard it, just a moment later—the rustle of foliage in a unified sweep toward us, some unseen enemy patrol coming from our front. The sound of their movement was close, and I was certain that they had either walked directly over Worthy or were about to step on him.

But the noises swept to my left side, perhaps ten feet away through the jungle, headed southwest. The movement of brush was joined by the scrape of metal on fabric, boots traversing muddy jungle, and the clank of magazines in loose equipment pouches.

If my team had been moving in anything but single file we'd have been compromised by now. Given the size of the element passing us, that confrontation would have been catastrophic—this must have been a squad-size element, ten or twelve men by the sound of it, and we'd accomplish little but breaking contact at best and being wiped out at worst.

The enemy patrol continued out of earshot, continuing their sweep southwest until their movement gave way once again to the countless songs of insects and amphibians chanting in the night. Pinching my eyes shut, I waited another ten seconds before Worthy spoke over my earpiece.

"Sorry about that, David. Couldn't see them until their lead guy broke brush a few feet away."

I brushed a stream of sweat away from my brow, feeling a flicker of doubt—had Worthy missed something that a more senior point man would have caught, or had he done as well as anyone under the circumstances? Either was possible.

As I prepared to transmit a response, I heard an African American voice over my earpiece. The accent was so authentic, so perfectly rehearsed, that it took me a moment to recognize the speaker as Reilly. "You're ghostin' us, motherfucker. I don't care who you are back in the world, you give away our position one more time, I'll bleed ya, real quiet. Leave ya here. Got that?"

Another Predator quote—ill-timed, to be sure, but at least morale was still high.

Cancer spoke next, addressing me. "That wasn't the only group of shitheads out here, David. We don't get ahold of this flyboy, it's a matter of time before we get in a gunfight. And I like shooting fuckers as much as the next guy, but that ain't gonna help the pilot."

"Yeah," I agreed, "let me try him again before we continue movement. Hang on."

Switching my grip to my command radio's transmit button, I sent another transmission over the survival frequency.

"Beast Three Six, American ground unit is due north of the crash site. Send your location."

I heard nothing in response, and considered repeating the transmission before we continued moving. We should have had the broadcast range to reach the pilot's survival radio, plain and simple. It was possible that he was hearing us and merely unable to respond—though that was unlikely. Even if he was transmitting in the blind, Ian should have been able to pick up his traffic and relay to us. I tried to think what I'd do if I were in the pilot's situation.

And after a few moments of consideration, the answer came to me.

If I were flying over an enemy-held island with no reported American troops and then shot down only to receive immediate radio contact asking for my location, I probably wouldn't respond either. The pilot could hear us, I decided.

He just didn't trust us.

I keyed the mic, and transmitted to the pilot one more time.

"Listen, brother. In a few hours this island's going to be

swarming with American forces trying to find you. But you don't have that kind of time." I momentarily released the radio button, then keyed it once more. "Think any of these terrorist assholes would know your unit motto? Well, I do. NSDQ— Night Stalkers Don't Quit. Now I've got a team of Americans ready to retrieve you, and your odds of leaving this island alive are low even with us at your side. Without us, they're zero. Give us a location, and we'll move to you."

Radio silence. I wiped the burning sweat from my eyes with the back of my hand. My throat felt constricted; if this pilot didn't believe me, then he was doomed. And we probably were too, because we wouldn't stop looking for him—but in this jungle, the odds of finding anything but an enemy patrol by accident were slim to none.

Then, a voice responded.

It was garbled, virtually unintelligible with static—but I could make out a string of numbers. Programming them into my GPS, I saw the eight-digit grid was three hundred meters northeast of our current location. That was no small distance in the current terrain; but we now had a fixed point to move to, and the enemy didn't.

"Good copy," I replied. "Stay put. We're headed to you, ETA forty minutes or so depending on terrain. Stay hidden until we get there—we're a bunch of gringos in native garb, carrying American weapons. You won't miss us."

A static-filled, unintelligible response came and went before Worthy's voice came over the tactical frequency.

"I copied all, David. What are we waiting for?"

We were on the move again in seconds. The terrain hadn't gotten any easier to traverse, but now I felt invigorated, covering ground as easily as if I were floating over it; for the first time, we were heading to the surviving pilot's known location. We didn't know who he was, but an American on this remote island was as good as a family member in danger.

And even under the current circumstances, the pilot probably didn't realize how much danger he was in. Because based on our location on Jolo, the man responsible for hunting him was the most dangerous man on the island—and now that he'd taken down an American helicopter, probably the most dangerous man in the Philippines.

His name was Khalil Noureddin. Unlike many of his terrorist contemporaries, he had no reason to pursue a life of violence—and that was what scared me most about him.

Khalil had been born to an affluent Christian family in Manila, and attended the University of London on full scholarship. And there, due to circumstances that no one seemed to know, he'd converted to Islam and assumed his current name.

Instead of returning home to Manila, he'd traveled to Jolo Island to join the ranks of Abu Sayyaf.

This was a confounding move. Any number of international terrorist organizations would have welcomed a Western educated convert with open arms; Abu Sayyaf, by contrast, was a homegrown movement whose strength lay in its family ties. Since its inception, it had largely disintegrated into a militant group interested in self-sustainment. Many in the ranks of modern Abu Sayyaf were bloodthirsty kids—sure, they managed a little Islamic rhetoric here and there, but for the most part their decision-making was a binary equation of ransom money or beheading.

But Khalil had inexplicably chosen to join his local terrorist movement, surely recognizing that his odds of being accepted in the insular power structure were close to nil.

And against all odds, he'd managed to gain a growing audience of loyal followers. Before tonight, Khalil Noureddin didn't warrant mention on the international stage of terrorist leadership, much less Defense Department-sponsored allocation of the top national military assets. Those elite units had their hands full killing or capturing the top global leadership, an endless cycle tantamount to cutting the grass.

My team existed to pull the weeds.

In a year, Khalil would have enough followers and security to protect himself against being targeted. But tonight, it only would have taken four men to slip into a jungle camp, kill him in his sleep, and vanish with nary a headline to speak of.

But we'd been sent in too late. One pilot had already paid the price for that, and now it was up to my team to ensure that the second made it home safely.

The sun was rising now, and we stripped our night vision to find the jungle equally green by day—though this brightness belonged to nature, not night vision. Lush vegetation exploded from all directions, from the undergrowth to treetops. Even the tree trunks were concealed by leaves or too covered by moss to disrupt the rich green around us, pierced only by the first golden beams of sunlight penetrating the canopy. Plumes of mist wafted across the streaks of light as the sounds of nighttime jungle were replaced by obnoxiously loud bird calls. Their shrill cries played chorus to the undulating chirps of forest creatures rippling through the underbrush around us, concealing our movement as we approached the pilot's location.

Once we were within fifty meters, I transmitted to the pilot.

"Beast Three Six, Beast Three Six, you should hear our movement any second. When you do, give us an audible."

I started to make out something gray to our front, its color alien amid the lush greenery shielding it. At first we only caught glimpses between the snaking tangle of trees, leaves, and vines, but as we pushed closer, we saw a water-soaked wall of craggy volcanic rock. It wasn't a unified cliff face but a formation of giant stones with vine-coated surfaces rising twenty feet skyward. We moved parallel to the rock face, keenly aware that an enemy force could easily pin us down against this impassable terrain feature. The pilot should have known that too and sought the densest possible vegetation, someplace where evasion would be possible in every direction.

Why would he risk hiding among these rocks?

Some of the stones in this formation were tremendous in size, jagged boulders with the scalloped appearance of hand-carved arrowheads. I spotted one sliver of darkness among the stone, then another. These were crevices leading deeper into the rock formation, their entrances partially shielded by creeping vines draped across the stone. Upon closer inspection, the entire primordial structure was pitted with innumerable shadowy crevices between boulders, some of them big enough to conceal a person from outside view.

Would the pilot have risked crawling into one of those, a certain dead end?

But the more I thought about it, the more hiding in one of these caves made sense. If you knew a rescue force was coming to your location, then it was a hell of a place to make a last stand. So too would that strategy explain the sudden absence of radio contact: the cave would have blocked the signal, requiring the pilot to transmit from the open before hiding again.

I keyed my radio. "Beast Three Six, we're here."

No response. We didn't have time to search every crevice, or hope he would hear the sound of our movement from wherever he was hiding, or even remain exposed here in the hopes that he'd eventually peek out and see us. If he wasn't going to give me an audible signal, then I needed to give him one—something distinctive enough to be detected over the cries of jungle animals competing for attention.

But what could that be?

I thought about what I'd want to hear as the lone American hiding amid hordes of enemy fighters, having narrowly escaped capture only to fearfully await the arrival of a supposed team of friendlies who had mysteriously contacted me on a survival radio.

And so I began whistling.

My tune merged with the throbbing chant of birds above us, detectable only between their calls.

Cancer momentarily lowered his rifle and placed a hand across his heart—I was whistling "The Star-Spangled Banner."

And while there was no lyrical accompaniment, my tune had scarcely crossed mention of the rocket's red glare when we heard a noise from the rock face before us.

I stopped whistling, trying to discern what I'd heard and receiving my answer when a pebble clattered down the stone surface and bounced into the underbrush.

Tracing the pebble's path upward, I saw movement in the shadows of a crevice and realized the pilot must have seen us before we saw him.

Then I realized I'd been wrong about one thing.

Because the figure clambering down the rock face toward us, clad in a digital camo flight suit and carrying a compact M4 rifle in the brightening glow of the jungle sunrise, wasn't a man at all.

It was a woman.

I switched my command radio back to Ian's frequency and transmitted, "Angel One, we've linked up with the pilot at known grid. Stand by for update."

Ian might have responded; if he had, I was too busy watching our newly found pilot descend the rocks before approaching my team. If I'd been a lone survivor in these circumstances, I'd probably be doing cartwheels toward my rescuers. But she was calm, unhurried, and looked surprisingly composed given the circumstances.

She was all of five foot four, with Latina features and dark hair pulled into a low bun. As I approached her, hazel eyes met mine with immeasurable gratitude as she whispered, "Thank you for coming."

I nodded. "Come on, let's push into some deeper vegetation so our medic can take a look at you."

Worthy led us fifty meters into the jungle, moving to a sufficiently dense spot for us to let our guard down without immediate fear of enemy observation. Once we stopped, he and Cancer picked up sectors of fire while Reilly dropped his assault pack next to the pilot.

She protested immediately. "I'm fine, really."

"Do I tell you how to fly helicopters?" Reilly asked. "I'm a medic. You were in a crash, and you're in shock. Or at least you should be. Let me take a look."

He checked her pupils, then had her watch his finger as he moved it left and right. Satisfied, he moved on to assess her for broken bones. His probing elicited a hiss of pain when he touched her left arm.

Reilly frowned. "Let's see it, tough guy."

She took off her survival harness, outfitted with aid and equipment pouches for just such an evasion scenario, and then unzipped her flight suit and pulled it down over her shoulder. The sleeve of her T-shirt was soaked in blood, and Reilly delicately lifted it to expose her slim tricep mottled in ugly purple bruising, the skin gashed apart.

Cancer looked over his shoulder at the wound and, unable to help himself, paraphrased a Predator quote.

"She ain't got time to bleed."

"Shouldn't you be pulling security?" Reilly hissed. Cancer looked away, and Reilly continued speaking to the pilot. "Bone's intact, so that's something. Just a nasty flesh wound I need to patch up." He began retrieving supplies to disinfect and dress her injury, then stopped himself and added suavely, "Name's Reilly, by the way."

The things about combat you can't make up, I thought—not a downed helo, or an injured pilot, or marauding enemy forces could keep Reilly from flirting.

But the pilot took no offense, seeming too relieved at the sight of Americans to mind.

"Josephine," she said. "CW3 Josephine Moreno. Where are the rest of your guys?"

"You're looking at it," Reilly said, pointing to each of us in turn. "David, Worthy, Cancer. Just the four of us. You make our fifth man. I mean, woman. Well, you know what I—"

I cut him off. "We saw the rocket volley from up on the ridge. I'm glad you're okay."

Josephine shook her head slightly, her eyes going unfocused.

"They got a lucky hit to our tail rotor. We autorotated our bird down, but the trees flipped us sideways. The impact killed my pilot-in-command, and he was—his body was pinned in the wreckage." Her nostrils flared, her breathing growing shallower as she continued. "I could hear them closing in. I made the decision to run. I zeroed out the radios, took my rifle, and...and..."

"You did the right thing." I placed a reassuring hand on her uninjured shoulder. "Every national asset is in motion to recover your pilot-in-command. Whatever you were doing flying a Little Bird over Jolo Island, I'm guessing you completed your mission by the time your bird got hit."

She said nothing in response to this, which didn't come as a surprise. Night Stalker aircraft usually flew in pairs, so whatever she was doing had been extremely discreet and thus highly classified. And while she may have trusted us enough to help her now, she wasn't going to reveal any operational details.

"So," I continued, "all we need to worry about now is getting you to the coast."

Now she looked at me with suspicion. "There weren't supposed to be any blue forces on the island. What are you people doing here?"

Reilly glanced at me and quickly looked downward, focusing on her wound once more.

Josephine continued, "I mean, your kit isn't cool enough for a JSOC element."

"Don't rub it in," Reilly grunted, wrapping a gauze dressing around her arm.

"So you guys are...who? Ground Branch?"

It wasn't a bad guess. After all, the CIA had technically sent us. But we'd never attended Agency training, much less served in the ranks of their elite paramilitary unit. The closest we'd legally ever come to CIA headquarters was a tenuous satellite connection.

"We're civilian contractors," I replied, handing her the hose to the water supply in my assault pack. She took a long sip as I continued, "We were conducting a routine island survey."

Josephine handed the hose back to me, and I began sipping water as she regarded me with a deadpan stare as if I was severely insulting her intelligence. Which, of course, I was.

"Contractors," she repeated. "Sure."

But she didn't press the issue, realizing the same thing I did: now, we were even. She hadn't divulged her mission, and we hadn't divulged ours—quid pro quo for the circumstances, and we both accepted that fact as well as the shared reality that the only thing we needed to concern ourselves with was making it to the beach before Abu Sayyaf turned us into five propaganda victories whose new standing height ended at the shoulders.

"What's your battle roster?" I asked her, referring to the universal military identification for use over the radio—the first two letters of last name, paired with the last four digits of social security number.

"MO2375."

I keyed my radio. "Angel One, we have linked up with pilot, battle roster MO2375. No major injuries. Currently fifty meters west of previous location. Request status of rescue forces."

Ian responded at once.

"Nearest carrier strike group with those assets is in the

South China Sea. They dispatched their Marine Expeditionary Unit in Ospreys as soon as the shootdown occurred. They're two hours out."

I winced. We didn't have that kind of time.

He continued, "The smaller amphibious group off your north shore has helos standing by, ready to air land in a clearing or drop a deep jungle penetrator through the canopy to hoist up the pilot. And they'll support that effort with helos flying false extractions on different parts of the island to divert the enemy forces."

This prospect was only slightly more appetizing than waiting, but still unfeasible given the volume of fighters here. They'd be drawn to an approaching helicopter like moths to a flame, and whether that bird was ours or a different one supporting the effort, one or more Americans wouldn't survive the outcome. Khalil had probably been stockpiling rockets for months to bring down a US helicopter, and there was no way he'd blown his entire wad the night before. The ground-to-air threat on this island was simply too great.

Reilly must have been thinking the same thing, because he paused his treatment to make eye contact and shake his head slowly.

Cancer looked over his shoulder and whispered, "No way, David. We head for the beach—fast. These Abu Sayyaf fuckers ain't gonna let us waltz to a landing zone, or let a helicopter hover for ten seconds without hitting it with everything they've got. We leave by boat, or we don't leave at all."

I reluctantly transmitted to Ian, "Negative. It's way too hot down here to wait, or call in a bird. We're going to break north for the coast. Request naval assets to loiter offshore for pickup."

"You got it, brother. Stay safe."

Reilly finished dressing Josephine's wound, and she zipped up her flight suit as we gave her a water bladder and a few energy bars to eat on the move.

I addressed the team with a concise mission statement.

"We're pushing to the north coast. Stay tight, stay quiet, and —I can't stress this enough—don't get shot."

The jungle seemed to grow hotter by the minute as we patrolled northward through choking levels of humidity. The heat didn't seem to bother the birds and insects whose daylight calls were every bit as loud as the nighttime creatures they replaced—and while they shielded the sound of our movement, they would also keep us from detecting all but the loudest approaching enemy until it was too late. Unlike our near-compromise the night before, we could no longer rely upon the cloak of darkness to help us evade overwhelming enemy forces.

Worthy remained on point, followed by me, then Josephine in the dead center of our file. Reilly was behind her, and Cancer brought up the rear of our formation. I glanced behind me, making sure we weren't moving too quickly for Josephine, and immediately realized that wasn't going to be a problem.

She looked like a new private with her M4 rifle, unaccustomed to ground patrolling but staying vigilant and keeping pace as well as any of us. I could tell she was pushing through the pain of the flesh wound on her arm, but her expression was resolute, jaw set in determination as she returned my gaze with a questioning shrug, as if to ask, what the hell are you looking at?

I returned my eyes forward with a smile. We wouldn't be able to lose her if we tried, I thought—even if we were compromised and broke into a run, she'd stick right with us out of sheer grit.

But I desperately hoped that wouldn't happen.

Now that we'd recovered Josephine, avoiding enemy contact was more critical than ever. The Abu Sayyaf fighters were still searching a huge radius around the crash site, unsure of which way she'd run—but if we compromised our position, Khalil Noureddin would send every jihadist shithead on the island straight to us. He knew as well as we did that the clock was ticking on our rescue. The US didn't fuck around when a servicemember was down behind enemy lines—they were currently sending every air, land, and sea asset screaming toward this island. Khalil would do everything in his power to capture a living US pilot in the interests of beheading her for a propaganda film before anyone could save her.

And if he rolled up an extra four Americans in the process, so much the better.

Worthy halted the formation, taking a knee and waving me forward.

I approached him to see the ground ahead turn from scrub brush to exposed roots and vines, their masses intertwined in dense formations that vanished beneath the gently rippling olive-colored surface of a wide stream.

The stream was about thirty feet wide, flowing briskly as it curved around our current location. We were at a bend in the stream—not much of one, but a bend nonetheless—and probably the best we'd be able to manage in limiting our exposure during the now-necessary crossing.

Worthy whispered, "Think this spot is good enough?"

"Obviously I'd prefer a tighter bend in the stream. But we can't risk the exposure of searching for one even if we had the time, which we don't." I keyed my mic and said, "Stream crossing. Bring Josephine up here and let's get this over with."

The other three advanced to Worthy and me, kneeling for a quick huddle.

I asked, "Can you swim, Josephine?"

"You kidding me right now?" she replied, looking insulted. "I'm a dunker jedi."

The "dunker" was more formally referred to as underwater egress training, where aircrews boarded a simulated helicopter that was inverted and submerged in a pool for them to find their way out of underwater. The Night Stalkers trained to do this in a blackout as well, which I supposed qualified Josephine to conduct the daylight stream crossing.

"Fair enough," I allowed, considering my next words carefully. In a traditional stream crossing, we'd send an advance force across to establish far-side security, then funnel everyone else toward them. But with five of us against a thirty-foot-wide body of water, we didn't have the manpower—and if our team got split on either bank by enemy contact, we were all as good as dead anyway.

"I say we go ducks in a row, spaced just far enough that we don't all get killed in a grenade blast. No near- or far-side security."

Cancer's brow wrinkled.

"You think? Fuckin' four of us."

"Five," Josephine corrected him.

He was undeterred. "I'll let you know when I find a helicopter out here for you to shoot missiles from. Until then, there's four shooters." He looked at me and said, "Come on, we're wasting time."

Worthy was the first in the water, probing tentatively with each footfall to assess when he'd have to start side stroking. But it appeared my concern for Josephine's swimming ability was unnecessary: halfway across the stream, Worthy's shoulders still cleared the surface.

I slipped into the water next, finding it slightly cooler than bath temperature and a welcome reprieve from the island heat. As I approached the halfway point, Ian transmitted over the command frequency.

"Send your location."

"Give me a sec," I replied. "Dealing with a stream."

"What side are you on?"

My blood turned to ice. "Right in the middle," I hurriedly replied. "We're crossing it now."

"There's an enemy patrol following the south side, headed east to west. If you can, get to the north—"

I spun toward the direction we'd come, pumping my arm in the signal to move faster. Josephine, a few feet behind me, registered the panic in my eyes. Reilly, already in the water, had apparently heard the transmission loud and clear—he had picked up the pace, closing the distance as quickly as he could.

But Cancer was the real loser.

He was just now rushing into the water, and for the first time since I'd known him, his face showed fear.

Before now I'd scarcely considered him capable of that emotion. Cancer was a borderline sociopath, with operational necessity representing the closest he'd ever come to even basic human morality. Whether he'd always been that way or had just seen so much combat that he'd shed his humanity like a cobra sloughing its skin, I didn't know. And the fact that this man was now wild-eyed with terror scared me more than Ian's radio transmission. Because a report of enemy movement wasn't enough to raise the hackles on a man like Cancer, nor was the prospect of his own end enough to trouble him. Instead he must have sensed something, if not heard or seen it, that made him realize death was bearing down on all of us.

And by the time I turned forward, increasing my own rate of speed as much as I could manage in the swiftly flowing water, I saw that Worthy was no longer headed toward the opposite bank.

Instead he was diverting left, having made a split-second judgment call to change course. His destination was now a mossy slab of volcanic rock over the stream, a pool of shadow across the water the only indication there was space beneath it. The rock overhung the water, but it was impossible to determine just how much space there was.

I had mixed feelings about this gamble—on one hand, we'd reach the rock overhang faster than we could feasibly clamber up the opposite bank and disappear into the vegetation. On the other hand, we could fight far more effectively on land, and we didn't know how much space was under that rock and whether some or all of us could fit.

But I'd chosen Worthy as our point man, and now we were committed to his choice. We'd succeed or fail together, and no sooner had Worthy reached the shadow beneath the overhang than he spun in place, aiming his dripping rifle above the water to cover our movement.

I paddled hard toward him, arriving into the shadow to find little more than a hollowed-out scrape of mud beneath my boots, the space requiring me to kneel with my head pressed against the rock surface.

By the time I'd lifted my rifle toward the far shore, Josephine was piling in beside me—the dunker jedi in action—and Reilly wasn't far behind her.

The only other movement I could make out was Cancer, who plowed across the water with his head turned away from us, keeping his view locked onto the southeast side of the stream where Ian had reported the enemy patrol.

It wasn't until Reilly had reached the overhang, squeezing in shoulder-to-shoulder with the rest of us, that I caught my first glimpse of the Abu Sayyaf fighters. There was movement in the distant brush, an unnatural rustling of foliage that immediately preceded the appearance of an enemy point man.

Cancer wasn't going to make it before he was spotted. I braced my rifle against my shoulder, flipping my selector lever to semiautomatic as I centered my optic on the movement. We'd have to open fire the moment an enemy point man spotted Cancer, and hope that the combination of suppressed fire and our concealed position would sufficiently confuse any remaining fighters into stumbling into the open before they could muster an effective response.

The last thing I saw before the enemy point man emerged

was Cancer. He spun his head toward us, now looking irritated rather than afraid.

Then he took a deep breath, and submerged himself beneath the rippling surface of the murky water.

I directed my gaze through my optic, seeing immediately that Cancer's disappearing act hadn't come a second too soon—the enemy point man was already clearing the brush on the far bank, paralleling the stream westward.

And mercifully, he didn't appear to have seen Cancer.

The point man was sunken-cheeked, looking like a moody teenager with long hair emerging from a bandanna around his forehead. Full-length M16 rifle carried at the low ready, with a Soviet-era chest rig bearing additional magazines. I'd hoped to see the complacency of a soldier anticipating a boring patrol, but this point man wasn't just alert—he was hyperalert.

He just didn't seem to know what he was looking for.

Instead his eyes darted around the jungle as if in the throes of a paranoid hallucination, looking at everything at once. His expression contorted with a series of facial tics, culminating in a rapid hand movement that I momentarily thought was him bringing his rifle to bear on us; instead, it was a jerky scratch at his fatigue shirt before he walked out of view.

Just when I thought he must have been a solitary fighter, I saw a second man appear in trail, then a third. Some were in fatigues, others in T-shirts of various colors. Their uniforms looked like they had marched through a Goodwill and put on whatever they could collectively find, with Arab-style thawb garments sprinkled in for good measure.

But they had guns, and lots of them.

Most carried old, stripped-down M4s or M16s, a few of them mounted with grenade launchers, and there were a fair number of rifles with heavier firepower—FN FALs, AK-47s, and even wood stock M14s chambered for 7.62mm ammunition. Judging by what I could make out across the stream, the weapons needed better maintenance than they'd gotten and the fighters needed better training than they'd received; but with the sheer volume of armed men on their side, Abu Sayyaf would be formidable in a direct gunfight. Some of these fighters had grenades dangling from their kit, and I sobered further when I saw a tall fighter marching with a crew-served weapon over his shoulders like he was starring in a Rambo movie. Upon closer inspection, I saw his weapon was an M-60 machinegun, and that piece alone packed enough firepower to ruin anyone's day.

I had counted twelve fighters when a heavy mass slammed into me beneath the surface. I jumped with fright before Cancer's close-cropped silver hair broke the surface beneath my rifle. What with all the commotion of a massive enemy patrol walking by, I'd almost forgotten about him completely. Josephine moved sideways to allow him to rise between us, and he exhaled a violent gasp before sucking in deep breaths of air.

"Quiet down," Reilly whispered, and Cancer's eyes went aflame with rage in the shadows beneath our rock overhang.

I tapped his shoulder and pointed to the opposite bank, and Cancer turned to see what we all did: a procession of enemy fighters with rifles and machineguns carried one-handed, at the ready, slung over shoulders.

Another of the young fighters was twitching spasmodically, slapping at his neck as he passed. He too was feverishly looking around the jungle as if expecting to die at any second, exactly as the point man.

I thought nothing of it until a third man in the formation exhibited nearly identical symptoms.

"What's wrong with those guys?" I whispered.

Cancer took another breath and said, "What's the matter, you never seen anyone on shabu before?"

"Shabu?"

"Crystal meth, dumbass."

Reilly defended me, whispering back, "Not all of us grew up

in Jersey. Don't get pissy because the rest of the US doesn't consider methamphetamines a food group."

Cancer merely shrugged, as if Reilly had a fair point, and the five of us watched the enemy patrol pass by—eighteen fighters in all—and disappear out of view as they followed the stream westward. I tried transmitting to Ian, received no response, and reached the fairly obvious conclusion that the slab of stone immediately overhead was blocking my signal.

We gradually made our way out from our hiding place, dripping water as we pulled ourselves up the root-covered bank and onto the north side of the stream.

As Worthy led us into the jungle on our way toward the coast, I contacted Ian.

"Angel One, thanks for the save. If you hadn't called when you did, we'd be floating downstream in pieces right now."

"Don't thank me yet," came his terse reply. "That patrol is moving to an unspecified crossing point, and will be sweeping toward the coast. You need to get as far north as you can, ASAP."

I gave a frustrated grunt. "When are you going to have some good news for us?"

"Not as long as Khalil Noureddin is alive. He must be mobilizing his men with a long-range radio—his voice is the only one I can make out clear as a church bell. Unfortunately, he's pretty good at this. Has his area of operations mapped out by sector, and he's trying to block off all avenues from the crash site to the coast. Thinks if he can contain you to the jungle, they'll find you before any responding forces."

"Well, he's fucking right. Can you jam his frequency?"

"I already asked the Navy. They have a pair of EA-6 Prowlers inbound from the carrier group, but they won't be here anytime soon."

Of course they wouldn't, I thought bitterly. "Copy. We're making our way north as quickly as our simple Southern point man can take us."

Worthy shot me a glare over his shoulder—he was still monitoring the command frequency, apparently—as I transmitted our current grid.

Ian replied, "Copy your location and direction of movement. Will advise if I hear any pertinent radio chatter."

The terrain on both sides of us now rose in elevated hillsides, and Worthy navigated the only feasible path northward, through the thick vegetation of the low ground between slopes.

This was, in a sense, counterproductive. The best move for our evasion would be to restrict our movement to the steepest, most inhospitable terrain. But to move uphill now risked hitting a dead end of volcanic cliff face, and with the eighteen-man patrol on our tail, that could quickly prove fatal. We were reduced to sharks fighting for air, forced to continue moving against the prospect of imminent death.

Staying in the low ground, of course, was a double-edged sword: if the landscape channelized us, it would channelize our enemy as well. We'd already taken on a three-man outpost, ducked a roving squad at night, found the pilot, and narrowly avoided contact with a daytime patrol six times larger than we were. That should have been encouraging, but my experience in combat told me the opposite. In reality, there was a very finite amount of good fortune to be had on any mission, and at present we were quickly running out of it.

No sooner had this thought crossed my mind than Worthy halted our formation. His whispered voice came over my earpiece a moment later.

"Hold tight," he said, "I can hear voices up ahead. Let me creep up and take a look."

"Copy," I said, turning to see the teammates to my rear collapsing for a tight 360 perimeter while we waited.

I approached Josephine, the only one of us without a radio earpiece, and quickly briefed her on the situation.

"Our point man hears voices up ahead so he's checking it out.

That patrol we ducked at the stream is crossing and heading north. Given the terrain, odds are good that they'll be right on our ass."

"Good," she whispered back, her brow beaded with sweat that flowed down her flushed cheeks. "I'm ready for some payback."

I regarded her with a begrudging sense of astonishment. Her reaction to this situation was idiotic and absurdly suicidal, which placed her in good company amid my team.

Worthy transmitted, "Looks like we got four guys taking a break right in the middle of our path."

"Can we wait them out?"

"Looks like a blocking position, fifteen or twenty meters from your current location. They're not going anywhere, and the slopes on either side are too steep to bypass without them hearing us. I think we're gonna have to take them."

A blocking position was a blessing and a curse—they were supposed to be containing us, which meant that Khalil likely considered their location the northern boundary of the enemy perimeter. If we killed them silently, we could make our final push toward the beach with some time on our side and, if we were lucky, few or no opponents in our path.

My team's reaction to this information was about what I would have expected. Cancer was nodding with the feral intensity that he exuded when gunplay was imminent. Reilly looked neutral, ready to get the job done to save Josephine.

"Copy," I transmitted back. "Keep eyes on. I'm bringing Cancer and Reilly to you. We're going to take down that blocking position."

Cancer and Reilly stood at once and began moving forward. But Josephine's eyes flared at my words, and her hand flew to my shoulder to keep me from rising.

"I'm going with you," she whispered, a Latina accent threading its way into her words for the first time since I'd met her. I could tell she was angry, ready for a fight. And after losing her copilot, she had every reason to be.

"Wait here," I replied. "That's final."

"I can shoot, you know. I'm a Night Stalker, not an airline pilot."

"It's not your marksmanship I'm worried about—"

"Oh, so it's because I'm a woman? You think I need protecting?"

Her nostrils were flaring, and I sensed Reilly and Cancer waiting impatiently behind me.

"Sister," I said quietly, "next time you want to run with the gunslingers, bring a can."

"What?"

I pointed to her rifle's bare muzzle and explained, "A suppressor. This blocking position has to go down silently. In the meantime, I need you to pull rear security while we move up. If we hear you shooting, we'll move to you. If you hear anything but suppressed gunfire up ahead, you come running to back us up. Deal?"

She deflated, realizing that I was right.

"Okay," she conceded. "And hey. If this turns into a two-way gunfight, you can count on me."

"If there's a two-way gunfight, I won't have a choice. Because if we get compromised now, we're all going to be fighting for our lives."

I held up my fist to her and she pounded it with her own, then spun and relocated to a tree trunk, crouching beside it and raising her M4 while watching our backtrail. The left sleeve of her flight suit was stained in an ugly red streak, the cut she'd sustained in the crash having already bled through Reilly's medical dressing. But to her credit, Josephine hadn't revealed the slightest indication that her injury would hinder her. Having seen her determination thus far, I didn't feel the slightest twinge of doubt about leaving her as the sole fighter on rear security.

I rose in place, finding myself under Cancer and Reilly's expectant gaze.

"All right," I whispered. "Let's go."

We advanced painstakingly forward, sacrificing speed for stealth until we found Worthy waving us in from behind a tree. Crouching down, we approached him and knelt for a quick huddle. By now I could hear people speaking up ahead, though I dared not peer through the bushes until Worthy said his piece. From our location, they sounded like they were conversing casually in Tausug. Someone let out a laugh, then quickly went quiet.

I leaned forward to hear Worthy, who was preparing to address us in unison.

But instead of his polished Southern lilt, he spoke in a crude Native American accent.

"There's something in those trees."

Another Predator quote.

"Goddamnit," I hissed. "Worthy, not now."

Worthy's eyes momentarily found the jungle floor, his voice returning to his normal plantation-owner brand of Southern. "Sorry," he drawled. "There's four of them from what I can see. All clustered in the low ground, fucking off. Bad visibility from down here, though. Recommend we cloverleaf back, then split up. Two guys up the high ground to the left, two to the right— we can't get high enough to bypass, but we can get better angles of fire before they hear us. Stop once we get visibility on the blocking position, then a coordinated slice and dice. The movement will cost us five minutes of prep time but really boost our chances of doing this thing quietly."

His eyes watched mine, and I tried to conceal a mild sense of surprise that Worthy had come up with what seemed to me the best possible course of action.

I nodded, then looked at the others. "Sounds good to me. Objections?"

Cancer shook his head, and Reilly whispered, "Let's do it."

"All right," I said. Worthy would need to stay with Cancer, the most seasoned team member. Reilly and I were in the middle ground of operational experience on the team, and we'd be fine together. "Cancer and Worthy go right, Reilly and I go left. I'll coordinate initiation over comms."

We backtracked five meters, then split into pairs. Reilly and I ascended a short distance up the west slope while Cancer and Worthy did the opposite, and then we converged on either side of the blocking position.

There was but a moment of high drama on our route to the final firing positions.

As I followed Reilly through the brush, some primordial instinct told me to freeze. I scanned the infinite leaves and vines around me, searching for a tripwire that had triggered my survival reflex before I'd consciously seen it—and while it took me a few seconds of heart-stopping terror to locate it, I found the source of my panic suspended from a tree branch just a foot away from my right cheek.

And it was no tripwire.

Instead I saw the emerald twist of a serpentine coil, its surface braided with scales and flecked with white markings. The snake's neck tapered to a narrow diameter beneath the wide, diamond-shaped head that faced me now. I saw smoldering eyes the color of burnt orange, the serpent as immobile as I was, poised to strike without so much as a flick of its tongue. Was it venomous? Why not. It appeared to be a pit viper, and given the way our luck was playing out at present, I wasn't going to win the lottery odds needed to find a harmless snake in this jungle.

Delicately retracing my steps in complete and total deference to the force of nature that had nearly ventilated my face with its fangs, I swung wide around the snake, then resumed my pursuit of Reilly in the lead.

I had barely resumed breathing before my mind returned to the next imminent danger: the four fighters below us, blocking our path to the coast.

I was nervous about taking our eyes off the small enemy force for the relocation, but with four of us, we didn't have a choice—there simply weren't enough of us to risk leaving a man in the low ground just to make sure four reportedly complacent enemies didn't move out. My anxiety mounted with each passing second as Worthy's estimated five-minute relocation time turned to six, then seven—but when Reilly threw up a fist for me to halt movement, then pointed through the trees down the slope and toward the low ground, I could see that the investment in time had been well worth every second.

The four enemy fighters were still there, all seated close enough to talk. One of them had stripped off his chest rig for comfort, and only two of them had their weapons close enough to fire at a seconds' notice—one cradled an AK-47 in his lap, another kept an M-16 slung over his shoulder. The other two had left their rifles in the leaf litter at their feet, arms wrapped around their knees as they chatted without a care in the world. They weren't expecting any opposition, and they were going to pay dearly for that assumption. I could make out a few hand grenades on their kit, but no crew-served weapons.

I nodded to Reilly and then transmitted to Cancer and Worthy, now undetectable on the far slope.

"I count four—ordered from left to right, men number one and three are closest to weapons and get the first shots. I don't see a radio, so no additional priorities of fire. We'll work left to right, you guys work right to left. Am I missing anything?"

Cancer responded, his Jersey voice sounding distant and tinny over my earpiece.

"Number four man has the radio on the ground next to his

boot. We'll clean him up after dropping the number three man. Ready when you are, boss."

Reilly had shifted position to brace his non-firing arm over a piece of deadfall, then laid the stock of his HK416 over his open palm and whispered, "I've got a bead on number one. He'll get a headshot."

I knelt into a supported position, centering my reticle on the number two man's center mass. Keeping a hand on my rifle's pistol grip, I used the other to transmit.

"Standby, standby. Initiation in five. Four. Three. Two. One. Initiate—"

The twirp of Worthy's suppressed fire punctuated my last two words, and I released the transmit button to reinforce my grip as I unleashed a trio of shots at my designated man. He was unquestionably hit, spiraling out of sight through the leaves as I searched for other targets.

I could see a man on the right sprawling into view, and drilled two rounds into his chest for good measure before continuing to sweep for survivors. For a moment all four men appeared to be down, and I broke my grip to transmit the order for us to converge on the low ground in a final assault.

And that's when everything went to shit.

A bloodcurdling cry erupted from somewhere in the blocking position, and through the leaves I saw my number two man stagger back into view. He had somehow gotten to his feet and recovered his AK-47, and was now wheeling it wildly before being hit by a half-dozen rounds from our two firing positions and falling out of sight.

"Maybe they didn't hear that," I transmitted hopefully.

Suddenly he burst into view again. He ate more rounds as we all re-engaged, desperately trying to shut down his central nervous system. But he was pirouetting across the low ground, changing direction like a jackrabbit. This guy wasn't just on crystal meth, I realized in a flash of panic—he was tweaking out of his mind, his vital systems persevering against all ballistic odds in a drug-induced overdrive.

I silently prayed with each round I fired. Headshot headshot headshot...

He spun, wielding his rifle in one hand as the other reached for a grenade. A round through his side caused him to whip around and, in the throes of death, rip a chattering automatic burst of fire from his AK-47.

Finally his head exploded and, dead at last, he spun sideways and fell to the ground. The echo of his gunfire receded into the jungle.

"Or that," I said.

Suddenly a grenade beneath his body exploded, sending his corpse momentarily skyward before he collapsed in a heap amidst a black cloud of dirt and incinerated leaf litter. That tweaker sonofabitch had managed to pull a pin before he gave up the ghost.

I keyed my mic a final time, the deep booming echo of the grenade rolling across the jungle as I concluded, "You know what? Maybe we should consider ourselves compromised, just to be safe."

Cancer replied, "Right side moving."

Reilly and I crashed downhill, pumping subsonic rounds into the visible bodies and reloading as we moved. I heard the chuffing of suppressed fire from Cancer and Worthy on the opposite slope before I saw them, and by the time we spilled into the low ground, there was no question that we'd bagged our four men—but the damage was done.

There was a crash of brush to our south, and I whirled to see Josephine emerging from the leaves.

"Sounds like that went pretty well," she said, appraising the bodies and then looking at me. "So, how'd those suppressors work out?"

Before I could answer her, the nearest enemy fighter writhed on the ground; whether due to the last vestiges of life slipping away or a postmortem twitch, I didn't know and didn't have time to ascertain. Josephine raised her M4 and shot him three times, then advanced toward the body to deliver a fourth round to his face at near point-blank range.

"Oh..." Reilly gasped shallowly beside me, his voice shuddering with desire. "I like her."

"Suicide, Suicide," came Ian's urgent voice over the command frequency. "Get moving. Someone heard you guys; Khalil is directing everyone to block the coast north of your last reported position."

We hastily stripped the grenades and compatible magazines off the enemy bodies. I left the lone enemy radio where it lay—it had taken either a ricochet or a direct hit in the melee, and the resulting bullet hole marked it inoperable.

Then we were on the run again, Worthy threading a path through the jungle as we resumed our order of movement and struggled to follow him in a tight file.

The jungle seemed to be screaming now, birds shrieking at us from all directions louder than ever; but I knew this was in my head, now ringing with the grenade blast, with the physical exertion of hauling ass north, with the hopelessness of our situation.

There were a few tactical plays we could make. Boobytrap the dead bodies with grenades so our pursuers would eat a blast as they rolled over their comrades. Move up the slope and stage an elevated ambush for the forces racing through the low ground behind us. Climb to high ground and hope the Marine Expeditionary Unit arrived before we were found.

But we knew the truth: each of these options would merely delay the inevitable. Our only salvation lay in reaching the coast; everything else was a false prophet.

We jetted north across the low ground, the plant density moderate but negotiable enough to move at a decent clip. To either side, the slopes rose steeper—we were still in the narrow pass, and Khalil had been smart to put a blocking position here. At this very second, he was undoubtedly redirecting forces northward of wherever this channel of low ground opened up, as well as sending patrols racing up our backtrail. If we found a dead end up ahead, we'd be forced to fight our way to high ground while picking off pursuers scrambling up the slope behind us.

"Angel One," I transmitted on the move, relaying our current location. "We're passing through a ravine now, need to know what we're facing up ahead."

There was a pause, and then he responded, "You'll be out of that low ground in a hundred meters or so—not much high ground after that, you're getting too close to the coast. Khalil routed most of his forces around the hills to the west, so advise you shift direction of movement from due north to northeast as soon as you're able."

Ian, of course, was right. The hills beside us tapered downward as we proceeded, the terrain leveling out to allow movement across a more or less 180-degree swath to our front. As we exited the pass and Worthy shifted our route to the northeast, I could make out the sound of movement and men shouting to one another somewhere to our immediate west—the enemy had rounded the hill just as Ian said they would, and now Khalil was trying to head us off at the pass before we could make it to the jungle beyond.

We were slipping the noose, but just barely—and any relief at this epiphany was snuffed out by Cancer's voice transmitting over my earpiece.

"I can hear people moving to our six o'clock. They're close."

"Well," I replied, "they're going to have to get in line, because we've also got bad guys to our west."

We hit a small strip of clearing, the jagged break in jungle stuffed with tall grass and extending in a narrow streak in either direction. Twenty meters of total exposure in a linear danger area, and no time to bypass.

"Bust it," I transmitted to Worthy, indicating to charge through as quickly as possible. This was a reflex order as much as anything else. We were five Americans with limited ammo and heavy pursuit by overwhelming enemy forces; it wasn't as if we had much choice.

The clearing was a sun-rippled expanse, and our team spilled into it with the desperation of foxes fleeing the hunt. We poured on a burst of speed to get back into the trees as quickly as possible—after our flight through the jungle, the blazing sunlight seemed hostile, the short plants aflame with a golden glow that exposed us unforgivably.

Low palms, ferns, and long blades of grass whipped across our bodies as we charged across the clearing, waiting for the sound of gunfire to explode behind us. My mouth had turned to sandpaper, the hot island air surging through lungs that burned with sheer exhaustion. I tried to run faster and found that my unsteady legs had no more speed to give.

I wildly searched the far tree line, scanning for our enemy's shadows before they saw us. If we didn't take fire now, it was because Khalil hadn't yet had time to maneuver forces into our direct path—and apparently that was the case, because we passed through the sunlit clearing without incident. By the time we finally reached the familiar encapsulating vines and thorns tugging at us as we moved, the jungle felt safe, serene, secure.

But like most victories on the island so far, this one was short-lived.

At first, everything seemed perfect. We slipped into a protective grove stuffed with tall plants that shielded us with their broad leaves yet allowed us to pass between the stalks and trunks with relative speed. Since the enemy had no concerns about noise discipline as they shouted to each other—a benefit of outnumbering your quarry by twenty-to-one, I supposed—

we could hear our pursuers behind us, while they couldn't hear or, for the time being, even see us.

But this grove ended in a short rise that Worthy clambered up, stopping mid-step to direct his attention downward. I saw what he was looking at before he sidestepped around it, and I wouldn't have put a boot down there, either.

Under other circumstances, that curiously formed accumulation of leaf litter between fern leaves would have appeared a poorly hidden boobytrap or landmine. Could it be natural? Sure, in theory. But the balance of evidence for such a piling rested heavily in favor of unnatural and thus man-produced, and no point man worth his salt—and Worthy had definitely earned his keep thus far—would dare place a footfall on such a risky and preventable misstep of chance.

So he rerouted around the pile instead, taking a few steps uphill to gain visibility over the other side of a small ridge. At that moment, I heard a voice shout in Tausug from the other side.

Whoever it was must not have seen us because Worthy didn't open fire.

Instead he tried to get out of sight, reversing his direction of movement with all the grace of being electrocuted as he backpedaled down the slope. But the jungle floor was loose with a blanket of rotting leaves, and he tumbled awkwardly down the rise in a wild, careening retreat.

In his hasty backpedal, Worthy managed to step directly onto the suspiciously abnormal-looking pile of leaf litter—the same one he'd gone out of his way to avoid moments earlier.

And then Worthy, to put it mildly, disappeared.

I'd never seen anyone vanish in such a flash short of them being blown up by an IED. This time, however, there was no noise other than a hollow whoof that signaled we wouldn't be seeing Worthy anytime soon.

Other than that, he was gone—but so too was the suspicious

pile of leaves. I darted forward, kneeling to peer beneath the ferns.

In place of the leaf pile was a black hole.

There, gazing into the black abyss, I realized a momentarily convenient truth: the volcanic rock formations that had shielded Josephine from view in the cliff formation operated below the surface as well.

I shined my rifle's taclight down into the jagged, manhole-sized hole, seeing Worthy lying on his back ten feet below, shielding his eyes against my light.

Turning in place, I furiously waved at Josephine, who was now standing, momentarily stunned, a few feet behind me. I could hear voices on the other side of the ridge growing in volume as they approached, and not even daring to whisper, I urgently pointed toward her, then the hole.

To her credit, Josephine didn't hesitate.

To the contrary, she actually shoved me aside, forcing me to catch myself with an outstretched hand before my shoulders struck the forest floor.

By the time I registered that she'd made it into the hole, her actions were repeated in short order by Reilly, then Cancer, as both swept the ferns away and disappeared inside.

Within seconds I was alone on the surface, listening to the enemy fighters approaching to our front. Staggering to a kneeling position, I shuffled closer to the hole, dangled my legs over the edge, and pushed myself over.

Ten feet doesn't sound like a lot. But when freefalling into a black void, I will hastily assure you it is.

Fortunately, I didn't hurt myself on a dreaded rock pile. Instead, I landed on the obvious—a heap of human bodies.

We untangled ourselves quickly, moving out of the human dogpile beneath the jungle's surface.

I found my entire team in a subsurface cavern; not much of one, but a cavern nonetheless.

The rocky space around us, momentarily illuminated by rifle taclights before falling dark again, was only big enough to hold fifteen men shoulder-to-shoulder before becoming untenable. Since our collective element was a third as large, it was overly sufficient—at least for now.

Amidst my team's grunts and groans, I stood on a spongy dirt surface and whispered, "Everyone okay?"

A muffled, grunted series of positive responses followed as everyone stood alongside me.

I looked up.

The sole light source now came from the oblong hole above us, dim sunlight streaming through the fern leaves that shielded it from outside view. That narrow channel must have become clogged with leaves over the course of months or years, until Worthy's body plunged through like a human chimney brush.

It would take an enemy fighter walking on top of this position to find us—but regrettably, that was exactly what was going to occur unless we figured out some better solution in a hurry.

I stood beneath the hole, trying to raise Ian over my radio to give him our current location.

No response.

"All right," I breathed into our huddle as the others closed around me, "even if we manage to break the enemy perimeter now, Khalil Noureddin will just maneuver his forces to cut us off. He's been doing a helluva job so far. Anything I'm missing on that assumption?"

No one objected.

"So the only way out of here is to take out Khalil."

"Sure," Reilly said, "and if we could channel lightning strikes with our minds, that might mean something."

I swallowed hard. "The enemy positions we've cleared so far have both had cheap, short-range radios. They can't transmit over distance, so they're mainly used to receive transmissions from Khalil. He's the brains of this operation, and he's the only one with a long-range radio. With the prospect of killing or capturing five Americans slipping away with each passing minute, he's not going to risk losing signal to his men."

Worthy asked, "So?"

"So," I began, "remember that sliver of clearing we ran through a few minutes ago? That's the only clear sky anywhere near us. As long as he can't hear any US aircraft, he's going to set up right in that clearing and maintain the farthest possible communications with his force."

Worthy said, "So you're proposing we slither back to that clearing and try to get a shot on Khalil before someone steps on us?"

"Not us," I said. "Me. Five people are tough to hide. One has better odds, and if—if—I can take out Khalil, we'll have eliminated all effective pursuit. We can punch a hole in the enemy perimeter, and then make a final run for the coast. I mean, our only alternative is waiting down here."

"Waiting ain't an option, David," Cancer said from the darkness. "We got fifteen, maybe twenty minutes at best before some shithead stumbles on this hole and drops a grenade in. Marines won't be here that fast. So let's say you succeed—how are we going to know? We won't be able to hear your suppressed fire, and we can't receive radio transmissions in this hole."

"Give him a grenade," Josephine said. "If we hear a single grenade blast, we know to move. If we hear a bunch of unsuppressed gunfire, we know we're on our own." No one replied, and she added, "Is that a dumb idea? Sorry, you guys figure it out. You're the ground fighters, not me."

I said, "That's a terrible idea, Josephine. Which pretty much lines up with everything else about this plan. Give me a grenade."

Cancer passed me one in the darkness while speaking in a haunted Native American voice.

"There's something out there waiting for us. And it ain't no man." Pausing for effect, he concluded matter-of-factly, "We're all gonna die."

"Goddamnit," I snapped. "That's the last time we watch a classic 1987 science fiction action film in the team room—I mean it this time. Though to be fair, pretty appropriate timing." I stripped off my GPS, handing it to Cancer. He accepted it without a word, figuring what I had: the last thing we needed was for me to get rolled up and for them to follow the GPS track back to the one spot on the island that was giving us even a momentary reprieve.

Then I said, "I'm out of here. If my grenade goes off, make a break for the coast as quick as you can."

"What about you?" Josephine sounded troubled.

I cleared my throat. "If I survive taking a shot against Khalil, then I'll catch up with you guys. Don't wait for me. Just make it to the beach. Now give me a boost, before I lose my nerve."

My team assisted me, and I felt their bodies bracing against the cavern wall, their outstretched hands providing footholds and support to hoist me toward the jungle surface.

The sunlight seemed blinding after the darkness of the hole, and I scanned the ground beneath the ferns that shielded this portal from above. No enemy boots in immediate eyesight, and my next step was to listen for voices—getting killed was one thing, but I couldn't afford a misstep that would compromise my team's location. But our hiding spot had precious little time remaining until it was discovered one way or another, and the second there was no human sound amid the birds shrieking overhead, I braced my arms on the moist leaf litter blanketing the mud around me.

Hoisting myself to surface level, I cradled my rifle in the crook of my arms and began high-crawling away from the hole on my knees and elbows. My sole advantage was the density of vegetation around me, but that narrow margin of fortune would evaporate as enemy fighters closed in. If they didn't discover me, they'd discover my team, and at this close proximity, one was as bad as the next. But with the collective hours of pursuit, my filthy fatigues were already blending as well as they ever would.

A sudden flash of color next to my face caused me to freeze in horror. A huge flat centipede emerged from beneath the leaves, its armor-like body segments kept in motion by twin rows of bright orange legs that clattered away from me.

Well that was fucking terrifying, I thought as the seven-inch-long venomous creature disappeared around a rock. Its sudden appearance had sent my heart into wild palpitations of fear, making the prospect of confronting armed men seem less daunting by comparison. I continued moving.

At least the vipers would be in the trees, I thought. Or at least hoped.

Crawling low, I moved the direction we'd come until the vegetation broke into spotty patches ending in the narrow clearing we'd just crossed.

Scanning between the trees, I crawled forward until I glimpsed sunlight marking the clearing ahead.

It was a view, to be sure, but not much of one: merely a narrow strip of visibility in the high grass that would give me a fleeting look at enemy fighters. Getting a view of Khalil here would be a moon shot, but if I moved much closer, I'd be found and killed at once.

My neck began burning with the impossibility of this situation. I assumed a prone firing position nonetheless, adjusting my legs and feeling a bulky object in my right cargo pocket bang against my thigh. Momentarily confused, I patted my pocket and realized it was the enemy radio I'd snatched at the small campfire on our way to Josephine.

I'd almost forgotten that I was still carrying it. But now, driven by despair, I desperately hoped it could be our salvation.

Retrieving the radio from my pocket, I considered my next move.

The power and volume knobs on this short-range radio were one and the same, and I rotated the knob just one click counterclockwise, then another, until the small screen came to life with a frequency and I heard the faint chatter of enemy transmissions in Tausug.

Then I transmitted to Ian, whispering over my command net, "Angel One, Angel One."

Ian answered, "Go for Angel One. How are you guys holding up?"

"Not incredibly well. I need to relay an enemy frequency from a radio we captured."

"Send it."

I gave him the frequency, concluding the numbers with the whispered and infinitely hopeless request, "Can you track that frequency and get us any more info?"

Ian's response in my earpiece was the last thing I wanted to hear under these circumstances.

"Sorry, brother. That's the same frequency I'm already monitoring."

Of course it was. We hadn't been able to catch a break since stepping out of the stream. It was just as I'd thought before—there was a finite amount of good fortune in combat, and in redirecting our efforts from killing Khalil to throwing ourselves into the fray in an attempt to rescue Josephine, we'd wrung out every last drop of our luck in the Philippine jungle.

Now we'd pay the price for that, one way or the other.

"Copy," I told Ian, "no sweat. I'll figure something out."

But what that would be, I had no idea. Based on the fact that the enemy wasn't stepping on me at this second, I could reasonably conclude that I was outside of Khalil's immediate security, yet well within the perimeter he'd established to contain us. Those perimeter forces didn't concern themselves with Khalil's safety, and his personal entourage wasn't concerned with finding the pilot; in between was a narrow bubble of complacency, and that's exactly where I'd positioned myself.

If I had Ian direct an airstrike against the clearing, Khalil would hear the birds coming and hide in the jungle. Even if I could miraculously summon the 360-degree firebombing of the jungle a safe distance from my team's position, the enemy was so close that many would be driven closer to us, not farther. And even if things got so desperate that I was willing to risk it, the carrier group aircraft hadn't arrived yet.

So what could I do? I didn't know, short of remaining in the prone and hoping for my enemy to stumble into view. I had to find a way to usurp the massive enemy forces here, to somehow pit my luck against Khalil's.

I scanned the clearing through my reticle, vaguely registering the quiet, tinny noises from the enemy radio—voices transmitting back and forth in Tausug.

Momentarily breaking my aim, I reached for the radio to turn it off. The absolute last thing I needed now was any further distraction.

Then something strange happened.

A single voice cut through the chatter, speaking first in Tausug and then in flawless English, an odd hint of British accent on his otherwise Filipino pronunciation.

"Cease all radio traffic. This frequency has been...compromised."

This was unmistakably Khalil Noureddin's voice, and I realized someone must have just discovered the three fighters my team had killed on our way toward the crash site—and the peculiar absence of their radio.

The next transmission sent my heart racing.

"I wish to speak to the leader of the team on this island."

My skin began to crawl, thoughts racing in disbelief at the obvious: I now had a direct line to the very terrorist leader my team had been sent here to kill. It was supposed to be an in-

and-out mission with no US affiliation and a minimum of one dead body in our wake; instead, we were now at the center of a military firestorm, downed pilot in tow, and it increasingly appeared as if we weren't going to make it out before the enemy found us.

I had no intention of answering Khalil. This was a short-range radio; it could receive transmissions from Khalil's long-range unit but didn't have the ability to transmit over long distances. If I replied, he'd know that I was in close proximity.

"I know you are listening."

I hesitated a moment, reasoning that engaging in a dialogue with a madman wasn't a good idea. But a voice inside me asked one question that I had no viable answer to.

Do you have a better idea?

I keyed the radio.

"You're right." I spoke quietly, just above a whisper. "I am listening."

"An American," he replied, sounding intrigued. "My name is Khalil Noureddin. And yours, sir?"

I transmitted, "Call me Suicide."

"Very well, Suicide. Let us talk business."

Keep him talking, I thought. Draw him into the open for a kill shot.

So I replied, "Speaking as a fellow businessman, I'm afraid I find your practices a bit concerning."

His tone was amicable, even polite, as he responded.

"My business practices emerged as all others: as a means to an end that fit my current resources. Your country appears to understand that principle quite well."

I swallowed, then keyed the radio again to ask, "And what's that supposed to mean?"

"Well, there are no publicly acknowledged Americans on this island. And yet from the current circumstances, I can only assume that when the helicopter went down, your team was already here to do business with me."

Well, I thought, this guy was no idiot. Demented and maniacal, perhaps, but no moron.

"That's an audacious assumption."

"I am in the business of audacity, sir. As I imagine you are. So I will make you a deal, from one businessman to another."

He still hadn't appeared in the clearing. I felt my throat constricting as the full absurdity of this plan began to take hold. My grand notion of sniping Khalil was going down in flames that grew in intensity by the second.

I tried to sound casual. "I'm listening."

There was a pause before he answered, though I could guess his offer. If we were going to die on this island, and the odds certainly seemed to be in favor of that, then we'd go down fighting. The proverbial blaze of glory seemed glamorous to people who'd never been to war, people like me when I'd joined the military out of high school. But once I'd cut my teeth in combat, I saw it for what it was: pure, unadulterated chaos. Any morals of patriotic righteousness or national policy hovered in a fog high above the battlefield, indiscernible to those in the battle who instead fought for one another.

So much the better, I thought. Maybe we'd accomplished nothing against Khalil, but at least Josephine wouldn't die alone. She'd fall beside her brothers, her fellow warriors who had risked it all to save her. And there was a virtue in that, a noble honor that was absent in much of the warfare I'd seen.

Khalil continued, "Consider the radio a token of mutual respect, and take it with you when you and your colleagues leave this island unharmed. I will have my people withdraw, and allow your safe passage anywhere you choose."

"Safe passage and a free radio," I mused. "Sounds good. What's the catch?"

"You have the pilot. Turn him over to my hospitality, and you will be freed."

I pinched my eyes shut, then blinked the sweat away as I scanned the sunlight in the clearing ahead. Khalil wasn't going to show himself; this was over.

"That last clause," I replied in a near-whisper, feeling my pulse quicken, "is a bit of a problem for my people. I believe our understanding of hospitality differs slightly from yours."

My breaths grew shallower as I began to hyperventilate. I'd tried to draw Khalil into the open and failed; instead, I'd have no choice but to rejoin my team and give the order to make one last-ditch effort to shoot ourselves free of the perimeter.

Except I knew what would happen immediately afterward. Khalil would quickly and effectively maneuver his forces, a calm and haunting voice over a long-range radio that could transmit to the bloodthirsty masses of enemy fighters now swarming around us. And we'd have no better chance of seeing the coastline than we did of waiting helplessly for some outside rescue to arrive.

Khalil responded, "These may not be the terms you hoped for. But I already have one pilot. My purposes would be better served by doing business with all of your people, rather than the remaining pilot alone. This is a generous offer, Suicide, and time for this negotiation is running out. You understand that much, if your whispered words are any indication."

And that was it, I thought—the whispered words. He knew I was still in range, and the fact that he could hear me whispering indicated his men were close to capturing me. Why should he bother to expose himself?

I stopped whispering, and gave my next transmission in a normal voice.

"Khalil," I said casually. "Time for this negotiation is running out. But not for the reason you think."

"Oh?" he asked, a sudden tinge of concern in his voice. He'd heard my increase in speaking volume, and his wheels were now spinning as he tried to ascertain how I could possibly have escaped his airtight perimeter. "Please enlighten me, Suicide."

"I'm making my own safe passage, with the pilot, right now. And we'll be off this island before you realize what happened."

I didn't key the transmit button as I spoke these words.

Instead, I pressed and released the button quickly, sending alternating syllables over the air as if I were headed out of range, moving beyond the reach of his receiver. As I did so, I watched the clearing with the pistol grip of my rifle firmly in hand, reticle centered ahead of me.

This was my last chance to draw him out, to make him fear that I was making a break for the coast, to goad him into re-establishing communications to continue our narrative. He hadn't broken cover into the sun-splotched clearing yet; maybe he would now.

And a moment later, I saw that my ploy had worked.

Well, "worked" may have been an overstatement. Because Khalil did break cover—I briefly saw a man pass my sights in the tall grass, trailed by an assistant toting a massive long-range radio on his back, following Khalil with the tether of the hand mic cord connecting them. But as I dropped my radio to take careful aim, they passed out of sight again, returning fleetingly to view seconds later as Khalil paced the clearing, trying to get reception.

My view was so limited that when they stopped moving, I didn't see Khalil but the radio held by his assistant, whose back faced me in a momentarily stationary position.

"Suicide?" he asked. "Suicide, can you hear me?"

I could take out the radio with one shot and leave Khalil alive, or I could hold my fire in the hopes that he'd expose himself for a fatal bullet. The odds for the latter were a matter of chance; for the former, a certainty. Or, I could be a moment away from losing them both altogether.

My gut instinct was to wait, to kill Khalil and accomplish the mission I'd been sent here to do—a grand slam of achieving everything at once. But then an odd voice spoke from the depths of my soul.

The mission was no longer to kill Khalil.

It was to rescue Josephine.

I pumped the trigger once in a precision shot, then fired three more times as quickly as I could.

The assistant and his radio dropped out of sight, and Khalil's transmission ended mid-word.

I dropped my rifle, grabbing the grenade from my kit. Yanking the pin, I hurled it toward the clearing. It wouldn't fall anywhere near Khalil, or even his security elements. But that was fine with me—all I needed was the noise.

It didn't come.

Shit, I thought, there goes our brilliant plan. Instead of a blast, I only heard men shouting from the clearing, realizing that they were no longer the hunters, but the hunted.

And then the grenade exploded.

The earth trembled beneath my body, the explosion creating a victory cloud of jungle earth and incinerated plants that expanded in all directions. It had the added benefit of obscuring the line of visibility from the clearing to my firing position, and I desperately needed that concealment as I pushed myself to my feet and began charging back toward my team.

To my rear, wild bursts of automatic gunfire erupted. I didn't break stride, instead juking a zigzag pattern between the trees, the jungle now providing a refuge of ballistic cover that I sprinted among as fast as I could manage. But it didn't sound like the gunfire was drawing nearer; the command element in the clearing probably thought they were under attack, and were therefore more concerned with protecting their leader and spraying my previous firing position with bullets than maneuvering toward potential danger.

Three grenade blasts erupted in the distance to my front. The crushing explosions gave way to gunfire of all kinds—long automatic bursts, to be sure, but also the precision fire of a disciplined shooter that could only be Josephine. I wouldn't be able to hear the rest of my team's suppressed shots, and that was just as well—the return fire gave ample indication of their current position.

I shifted direction toward the noise, hoping to link up with my team before they could make it too far. If they punched a hole in the enemy perimeter, I needed to run through it or risk hitting a wall of enemies too powerful for me to overcome.

Suddenly the noise ended altogether, leaving me to the slamming of my heart amid the panicked cries of birds now bursting through the treetops, fleeing the sounds of battle. It was at this moment, focused like a bloodhound on the last gunfire I'd heard, that I felt quite naked without my GPS. Leaving it behind had been the right move, but that didn't assuage my panic when I mounted a short ridge to see the carnage that my team had inflicted and realized they were gone.

Five enemy fighters were visible at a glance, their bloody bodies sprawled around a small, smoking crater where a grenade had found its mark. One corpse was half blown-apart from the blast, his body split and blackened; the others were peppered with debris and bullet wounds, two of them appearing semiconscious although they'd never again pose a threat.

I charged downhill, vaulting the grenade crater and continuing past them without bothering to clean up the site with fatal shots. Khalil could no longer control the countless enemy teams combing this area, but every dickhead within earshot would be converging on the fading sounds of grenades and gunfire.

And sure enough, no sooner had this thought crossed my mind than I saw the first responders to arrive.

They were coming from two directions—my left front and right front—probably two separate teams converging toward the noise. I saw the bushes moving before I saw the point men, desperately hoping to thread the gap between them before they saw me.

But patches of fatigues were visible through the leaves, seemingly in both directions at once. I swung my barrel to the right, popping four rounds and seeing that it did nothing to stop the advance. A suppressed weapon with subsonic rounds was a fantastic tool when moving stealthily, but in a situation like this, when my sole intention was to lay suppressing fire, it was of immeasurable disadvantage.

Simply put, these lead fighters didn't know they were being shot at.

I flipped my weapon to fully automatic, pouring a long burst at the fighter to my right. My wild spray thwacked through the leaves around him, scoring a lucky hit that sent him stumbling before I swung my barrel left to repeat the process.

The fighter to my left was now in the open, almost alongside me, the looming sweep of his AK-47 rising upward to deliver a fatal blast.

Rather than stop to aim, I pivoted toward him with a side-step, as if my goal were to run straight into him; when he encompassed my view, I mashed my trigger down while holding my HK416 at the hip.

This burst succeeded in cutting him down—he was gutshot, tumbling forward as I leapt away from him, my weapon now empty.

Then I was past them both, plunging into the jungle with the hope that the enemy I hadn't yet seen would be too momentarily confused by their respective point men's sudden, silent wounds to give rapid chase. I didn't have much choice—the time it would take me to appraise their intentions, much less reload my now-empty rifle, was too great to hazard. I stripped the magazine from my weapon, casting it aside and reloading on the move. There was no more thought of inflicting casualties on the enemy; my team and I were too close to the beach to worry about that now, our only true salvation residing not in the jungle but on the coastline.

Now I had no idea where my team was located, and no GPS to facilitate a link-up even with radio contact. But by the time it occurred to me to transmit to them, my attention was seized by a terrible sound from the high ground to my left.

A belt-fed machinegun opened fire, and for a moment I thought the opening salvo was going to rip me apart. There were no bullet impacts, yet the machinegun kept firing long bursts; any relief at my immediate survival evaporated with the realization that this gun was firing at my team, now somewhere in the low ground beyond.

I turned and made my way uphill toward the sound, vaguely registering Cancer's voice over my earpiece.

"—pinned down. Can you see him?"

Worthy answered, "Negative, they got me dead to rights."

I transmitted to them, "This is David, I'm inbound to machinegun, standby."

"Make it fast, David," Cancer said. "We've got a boat to catch."

Ungrateful bastard.

These guys had saved my ass before, and now it was my time to return the favor. There were few advantages to being isolated from my team, and I was about to cash in on the fact that the enemy didn't suspect a lone gunman roaming the woods behind them.

I approached the high ground, transmitting again.

"Hold fire, hold fire."

Cancer confirmed, "Holding fire; you're clear to engage."

But now I was summiting the crest, my HK416 at the ready, scanning for targets and seeing none as the machinegun bursts grew louder to my front. Clearing the side of a huge, moss-covered tree trunk, I saw the enemy team oriented perpendicular to my direction of movement—a gunner aiming a huge M-60 machinegun downhill as the man beside him fed a belt of ammunition into it, flanked by two men taking pop shots with their rifles.

Setting up on the left side of the trunk, I readied my carbine to eliminate a threat that had no idea they were about to die.

The era of a fair fight had ended, in my mind, with the departure of muskets from both sides of a battlefield. After that, warfare had become on the surface what it always had been to those who knew it: a free-for-all of might, tactics, and sheer audacity where the victor wasn't the most noble, only the most prepared and, in many cases, the luckiest.

Now I paused to take careful aim—I wasn't interested in finding out the hard way that anyone in this crew was high on meth and therefore endowed with superhuman strength. I centered my reticle on the back of the machinegunner's head, a single puff from my suppressor causing the view to be clouded with pink mist before I drove my aim to the man feeding a belt of ammo into the beast.

He was turning his head toward his gunner, now slumped dead with his brain matter frying on the scalding barrel. I drilled a round through his temple, and that was the end of any surprise I'd achieved by appearing unnoticed.

The first surviving fighter to realize what had happened whirled toward me, twisting on his side to take aim. This was no time for precision fire, and I sent a half-dozen rounds toward his form on the ground. The first bullet struck his pelvis, a heinous cry going silent as the remainder stitched up his midsection until the final round pierced his sternum head-on.

I heard a burst of rifle fire, the sudden crack of a bullet

piercing the still air next to my head serving as the second indication that I needed to get out of sight. Tucking my body behind the tree, I ducked to a knee and emerged from the opposite side, trying to dial in the last remaining fighter.

My view was of bushes and ferns, though to rise any higher would expose me to the continued gunfire from a man who was now shouting at the top of his lungs in words I didn't understand, a stream of Tausug in angry and panicked response to his teammates' sudden deaths. I aimed toward the noise, unleashing a spray of single shots through the foliage in the hopes that one would connect.

I never found out if I'd succeeded, but the gunfire stopped and, along with it, the shouting, the latter ending in a cry that trailed off miserably. He could have been wounded, dead, or merely given up, and I didn't bother sticking around to find out which. In the current circumstances I felt confident that whatever the outcome, he wasn't going to valiantly recover the machinegun and begin re-engaging my team.

I scrambled off the ridge, descending toward the low ground as I transmitted.

"You're clear, get moving."

Cancer responded, "Copy, we're picking up,"

I plunged into the low ground, my boots pounding against the jungle floor as I fought my way northward.

"I should be catching up soon," I transmitted. "Moving due north in the low ground—try not to shoot me."

Reilly answered, "Keep coming, we can hear your movement."

I burst through a patch of ferns, barely halting myself before what would surely be the last thing I ever saw: the muzzle of a rifle barrel leveled at my head at nearly point-blank range.

And Josephine was holding it.

She lowered her M4, panting breathlessly. "What took you so long?"

Behind her, Worthy was already turning to thread our course north to the shore, and I followed him as Cancer and Reilly stepped aside to resume our order of movement with Josephine in the middle of our file. That was the extent of our reunion at present, and seconds later we were on the move as if we'd never been separated.

And while this much was unquestionably a relief, I felt a sickening pull of dread as Cancer transmitted from the end of our small formation.

"We got movement behind us—need to pick up the pace."

They were already on our tail again, and I had to concede that Khalil was doing a remarkable job with only a glorified walkie-talkie—I shuddered to think what would have happened had I not removed his long-range radio from the battlefield.

Sunlight was now visible through the trees to our front, and I transmitted hopefully to Worthy.

"Tell me that's the coast."

"No," he replied. "Another clearing."

The jungle gave way to a sun-soaked clearing of sugarcane and plants rising to shoulder height. Why not, I thought—we'd covered kilometers of dense forest that hindered our progress, and here was a clearing where we wanted it least. The enemy didn't need to overrun us here, only wait at the forest edge and let the movement of brush in the clearing guide their shots. But we had no time to reconsider or circumnavigate this exposed area—we were running perilously low on ammo and water, our collective exhaustion rising with each passing minute. So we plunged into the green swath of plants, pushing hard through the whipping stalks and leaves, hoping to minimize our exposure time with speed.

It almost worked.

We'd reached the far edge of the clearing before we heard shots break out to our rear. Bullets hissed and snapped through stalks of sugarcane, and the moment Worthy and I reached the jungle, we took up firing positions to cover our remaining teammates as they made their way toward us.

I couldn't distinguish any fighters at the far side of the clearing, and instead pumped rounds at likely enemy positions as Josephine ran between Worthy and me, followed by Reilly. Cancer was last, and had just plunged past me before his body jolted with a bullet impact.

He stumbled forward and fell, crashing to the earth with a bloody wound below his right shoulder blade.

Reilly descended upon him as Josephine took cover to return fire. By the time I skidded to a halt and knelt beside Cancer, he was rolling to his side, pushing Reilly away.

"Get off me! I'm fine."

Reilly's eyes met mine, the relief evident in his face.

"Had to be a ricochet, or he'd be bleeding out now. He can move."

"Worthy," I shouted, "let's go!"

He stopped shooting, glancing to me in confusion.

"Ricochet," I explained. "Josephine, you're on casualty transport with Reilly. I'll pick up trail."

The low ground ended suddenly in an uphill slope, the worst possible scenario for a casualty, however minor. Worthy led the way unhindered while Cancer limped painfully, arms slung around Reilly and Josephine as they struggled to assist him up the slope.

There was no time to stop, or even think. The leaves and branches were whipping across our faces, but we forced our way uphill regardless—there was no time for hesitation, no chance to second-guess our decision. With the entire US military descending on this island, there was no question what would happen if we were captured. Because despite the translation of Abu Sayyaf—Bearers of the Sword—the preferred instrument of their trademark decapitation was a knife, making the process as gruesome as possible. The men chasing us would put the blade to our throats before any rescue was possible, and document the proceedings on video to herald their victory to the terrorist world at large.

Now the last person in our formation, I could hear men crashing through the brush behind us, shouting to one another and following our course uphill as they cleared the field in waves. I couldn't yet see them, but they were close enough for me to feel a compelling need to pause periodically, laying down a half-magazine of single shots toward the sounds of rustling brush and enemy voices before catching up with my teammates.

I transmitted to Ian, "Angel One, we're moving up high ground, coming in hot toward the shore. Be advised, we've got the Mongolian horde on our tail."

I ignored his response, instead keying the tactical frequency to transmit to my team.

"When we hit this high ground," I gasped, sucking for air, "let's flip around in a hasty ambush. Take out some front runners before we continue. I can't hold them off much longer."

I was pushing hard uphill, my lungs aflame when I heard Worthy's response.

"Don't stop, I can see the water!"

His last word struck me like a bolt of lightning, and I knew instantly what he meant—he could see the liquid horizon surrounding this island, and if that was true, we were so close to rescue that to stop now would be the height of insanity.

A second later I saw it too, the jungle suddenly parting to reveal sky and, beneath it, an endless blue sea.

Then my feet stepped forward to nothing, the earth sloping sharply downhill beneath me as I skidded into a rapid descent. I caught a blurred vision of Josephine and Reilly supporting Cancer's weight between them, struggling to keep their footing on the steep downhill slope. Worthy was speeding in front of them, casting a panicked glance over his shoulder that was probably as much out of concern that they'd fall and take him out on their way down as it was to see if I'd made it over the edge.

Then the world exploded over my head.

I felt the sky splitting above me, a distant deafening roar interspersed with the cracks of infinite machinegun volleys slicing through the air. A pang of fear gripped my chest—it was as if we'd summited the ridge only to encounter an entire army on the other side. Only my panicked glance below, toward the source of fire, assured me that we hadn't stumbled into an entire army.

It was a navy.

The dozen small gray vessels scattered along the coastline were American, and the gunners onboard were now raking the ridgeline above me with heavy machinegun fire in long bursts to ensure that any Abu Sayyaf pursuers found sufficient motivation to let their quarry escape.

I should have felt indescribable relief, but my concerns at present were solidly grounded in countering gravity's pull as I slid and bounced downhill, skidding and bumping on a slope of sand and rock ending in a narrow beach. By the time I came safely to rest on level ground, the massive concussion of machineguns firing on the ridgeline had ended altogether, fading to an echo as the gunners maintained their aim on the high ground above us.

And just like that, it was over—the combat action done, my heart still beating out of my chest with exertion, head ringing from the gun blasts and overall disbelief. We were on a thin strip of sand now, soft waves lapping the shore a few meters to our front.

By now, however, we knew not to push our luck on this island. Worthy, Reilly, and Cancer had already pivoted, sweeping their aim across the high ground alongside the Navy and Marine Corps gunners on the boats. I hurried Josephine toward the water, advancing toward the ladder of a small boat anchored in the waves awaiting her arrival.

Ian's voice came over my earpiece.

"Suicide, look to your right."

I did, and saw nothing but a palm frond blocking my view of the beach. Pushing it out of my way, I saw another vessel waiting in the shallow, wave-splashed waters.

It was an innocuous white fishing vessel, its paint chipped and battered. Surrounding it in a half-circle in the deeper water was a trio of small naval vessels, their guns trained toward the shore.

"Josephine," I said, stopping our advance toward the sea, "this is where we part ways."

She appeared confused, then looked past me toward the odd native vessel with a vanguard of US Navy boats. Her eyes met mine, and she appeared to understand everything at once.

Josephine didn't argue with me this time. Instead, she asked, "Well, what about when we get back to the States? How do I look you guys up?"

"You don't," I said. "You're going to be debriefed by some people from the embassy. They're probably going to make you sign non-disclosure statements. You evaded capture and made it to the coast by yourself, and you're going to get a valor award for your actions."

"Why do you say that?"

"Because I'm going to write you up for it."

She shook her head. "Why would I accept an award for something I didn't do alone?"

"Because," I concluded, "you're not just accepting it for you and your fallen pilot, which would be reason enough." I swept a hand toward the rest of our team—Worthy, Cancer, and Reilly, oblivious to the conversation as they directed their barrels at the jungled high ground. "You're accepting it for them, too."

She seemed to understand this, her lashes fluttering ove

hazel eyes.

"Well if you guys are ever hiring, I want you to look me up."

"If we're ever hiring," I said, "we will. Watching you shoot people was like watching a baby take its first steps."

Her face broke into a smile, then a laugh that ended with tears in her eyes.

I said, "Goodbye, Josephine."

"Goodbye, David," she replied, holding up her fist.

I tapped her fist with my own, and she walked off—but not toward the waiting Navy boats. Instead, she approached my team, fist-bumping the others in turn and exchanging a quiet word.

Then she was gone, walking away from us, down the sand and toward her waiting rescue. I watched her wiping tears from her eyes as she walked into the surf, into the waiting arms of two Marines who had descended into waves at the bottom of a boarding ladder, helping her up before the first one ascended after her. The second Marine was a huge black man who half-heartedly reached for the ladder, watching my team as if trying to comprehend what he was looking at.

Then he mustered himself to the position of attention in the water, snapping a sharp salute toward us.

I returned his salute, though I wasn't sure whether he saw it or not—he was already darting up the ladder behind Josephine, barely reaching the deck before the vessel backed into the deeper water, churning a long arcing turn toward the waiting amphibious fleet.

"You ready, David?" Worthy said from behind me. "Getting wasted on the beach by some sniper in the trees is a helluva way to go."

"Yeah," Cancer agreed. "Plus I need a smoke. In a bad way."

We helped Cancer painfully negotiate the short stretch of beach as Worthy shot up the fishing vessel's ladder, bracing himself at the top to help Cancer aboard as Reilly followed.

I was the last aboard, clambering up the ladder and onto the gently rocking deck as my teammates disappeared into the cabin to treat Cancer's wound. I made a move to follow them, then stopped abruptly and cast my gaze toward the horizon.

Josephine's boat was speeding away at maximum throttle, bouncing on the waves with its escort ships in tow, taking her back to the amphibious fleet stationed offshore. I braced myself against a guardrail as our fishing vessel slowly turned in the same direction and set off into the sea. The trio of Navy boats whirled around next to us, assuming a protective formation until we reached deeper waters. The gunners were still training their machineguns toward the shore. One of them watched me in between scanning the shore, and I gave him a thumbs-up. He returned the gesture, and I looked back toward the sea.

The sky was an endless cerulean expanse above a rippling seascape that stretched into oblivion. Mottled blurs of white cloud beckoned invitingly in the distance, assuring safety and comfort now that we'd left the terrorist hotbed of Jolo Island.

But I knew the truth.

We were mission failure on our first excursion, and for good reason. Khalil Noureddin would be flagged for life as the mastermind of an attack that killed a US pilot, and the best hunter killers on earth would pursue him until he was killed or captured. That put him well above my team's purview, and while I felt a tinge of regret that we wouldn't be the ones to bag him as I'd hoped, this loss was inconsequentially small against rescuing Josephine.

For my team, a different fate awaited. Because while Khalil had survived us for the time being, there were many other weeds to be pulled from the land of organized terror. We had cut our teeth in this new world, myself included. Khalil was our first attempt, but he wouldn't be the last. New battlegrounds awaited—provided my team wasn't disbanded in the fallout of this targeted killing-turned-rescue operation—and after the fate that nearly befell Josephine, we would be ready.

My thoughts were broken by Ian's nasal voice, suddenly audible not over my earpiece but directly behind me.

"Welcome back to the ship."

I turned to see his lean form, sunglasses dangling from the collar of a nylon shirt as if he were a tourist on a commercial fishing charter. His balding temples were concealed beneath the brim of a khaki boonie cap.

Ian's eyes were bright and joyful, and his wiry arms spread wide for a hug.

I grabbed his shirt with both hands, slamming him against the wall of the cabin as I shouted, "You set us up! It was all bull-shit—all of it! The cabinet minister, the whole business!" I lowered my voice to a growl, bringing my face closer to his. "Got us in here to do your dirty work."

From inside the cabin, I heard Reilly shout, "David gets the case of beer!"

"Goddamn right I do," I yelled back, releasing Ian and smoothing his shirt.

Ian blinked quickly, having been rendered silent in utter disbelief.

"My God, David," he finally gasped, "have you guys been doing Predator quotes...this whole time?"

"Yeah, pretty much."

"Points for consistency," he admitted, pulling me into a quick hug and slapping my back. "Come on, let's get in the cabin. Duchess is on the line for you—as you probably guessed, she's pulling us out of the Philippines ASAP. But she has another mission lined up."

"Well don't make me wait," I said. "Where are we going next?"

Ian sucked his teeth, then spoke in an almost reverent voice.

"Syria, David. We're going to Syria."

THE ENEMIES OF MY COUNTRY
SHADOW STRIKE #1

On a mission to assassinate a Syrian operative, a young CIA contractor uncovers a shocking terrorist plot that threatens his wife and daughter.

David Rivers is very good at killing people.

He's an expert in the art of violence—first as a Ranger, then as a mercenary, and now as a CIA contractor conducting covert action around the world.

But he's never had a family to protect...until now.

Newly married, and with a five-year old adopted daughter, David thinks his family is safe in Charlottesville, Virginia as he risks his life abroad. But when his mission to assassinate a Syrian operative reveals an imminent terrorist attack on US soil, nothing can prepare him for what he discovers.

The attack will occur in one week. The target is in his hometown.

And his wife and daughter are mentioned by name.

Get your copy today at
severnriverbooks.com/series/shadow-strike-series

Turn the page to read a sample.

THE ENEMIES OF MY COUNTRY: CHAPTER 1

Northwestern Syria

The Syrian horizon had gone from black to coral with the onset of daybreak, and now that the sun was beginning to lift skyward, it settled on a flame-orange glow.

I stowed my night vision device, rubbing away the phosphorescent green hues to see my surroundings through my own eyes—and as was all too common in my previous incursions into foreign countries, the land was staggeringly beautiful.

Windswept hills of rock and sand undulated as far as the eye could see. From my vantage point under a stone outcropping, the ground fell away to a dirt road slicing through the ancient stream bed below, the rocky cliffs lit with the sun's first rays. The air was brisk with the fading night, fresh with the smell of a new day ahead. This was a sunrise I would've liked to share with my daughter, with my wife, save one small detail.

I was in Syria, and neither my family nor any sanctioned military force knew I was here.

Ian spoke quietly beside me.

"We've got a ping."

I turned to look at him, his face softly lit by the screen of his tablet.

He continued, "This is it—BK is on the move."

I released one hand from the grip of my HK417, a heavy assault rifle chambered in 7.62mm. Normally I preferred working up close with a smaller caliber, but today's target called for longer range, greater penetration, and increased stopping power.

Keying my radio switch, I transmitted to the rest of my team.

"Net call, net call. BK has departed. ETA to kill zone six minutes. Cancer, stand by for visual."

***

Cancer watched the world beyond his crosshairs, a crystal image of the village in the foothills to the west, and offset his reticle from a building just under two kilometers from his position. He wouldn't be shooting that far today—not that he couldn't.

The sniper rifle tucked against his shoulder was the Barrett M107, a thirty-pound beast of a weapon that had been beyond cumbersome to haul up the rocky slopes to his current position. But now that he'd reached his perch, and was currently sweltering inside his ghillie suit, he had the ability to deliver a .50 caliber round into anything within a one-mile radius.

Cancer focused on a faraway single-story building, letting his eyes tick to the dirt road emerging from behind it. For now, all he needed to do was report the make and model of any vehicles headed outbound on the road that snaked through the rocky canyons. Then, when Ian had positively matched the trace of their target's cell phone to the vehicle in question, Cancer would have a few minutes to reposition himself with a line-of-sight to the kill zone.

And once the vehicle entered that kill zone, Cancer though

with a grin, he'd be able to unleash torrential hellfire. Auto glass, human torsos, engine blocks—nothing was a fair match for the Barrett.

Cancer's grin faded with his first glance of a vehicle leaving the village. He watched for a split second of disbelief before keying his radio to transmit in his Jersey accent.

"I've got eyes-on, ETA five minutes to kill zone, and...we've got a problem."

***

The apprehension in Cancer's voice made me uneasy.

"What's the problem?"

"*It's not one vehicle, it's three. All pickups, and they're moving in a tight convoy. Looks like five to eight armed fighters in the back of each truck.*"

I looked to Ian.

"Any chance that's not our guy?"

Ian shook his head, the veins in his balding temples standing out in stark relief. "Tracker is on the move—it's him. Probably in the center truck."

Cancer's voice came over the radio again.

"*What do you wanna do, boss?*"

I weighed the options. None were good.

We'd already burned an extensive Agency ratline to move our five-man team into position along this ambush point, awaiting what was supposed to be one vehicle carrying our target. The sudden presence of two additional vehicles and ten to sixteen enemy fighters wouldn't matter much in Hollywood, where every bullet found its mark and the bad guys all died when they were supposed to.

But if we carried out our ambush here in the Syrian desert, we'd better kill them all on the first go. If they managed to disperse on foot, they'd be able to kill us in a counterassault either immediately or as we tried to reach the vehicles staged for our escape. Letting them pass in the hopes of getting a better opportunity later would increase our exposure time amid extremely dangerous terrain swarming with too many armed militias to count.

I transmitted, "Worthy, hit the first truck when it reaches the chokepoint. Cancer, you've got engine block of the trail vehicle, followed by the center truck in the convoy. Ian and I will engage the center truck. Reilly and Worthy, you work front to rear. Questions?"

"*Got it*," Cancer replied. "*Relocating to get eyes on the kill zone.*"

A moment later, and with a touch of hesitation in his Southern lilt, Worthy replied, "*Racegun copies all.*"

Beside me, Ian muttered, "David, you sure about this?"

"Not even a little bit," I admitted, "but we're going to do it anyway."

***

From his vantage point on the eastern flank of the firing line, Worthy readied his M72 LAW with nervous anticipation.

The weapon felt light and powerful in his hands; it was a portable, one-shot rocket launcher designed for taking out a tank. Against an unarmored vehicle, the effects would be devastating.

At least, he thought, that's how it *should* have worked.

With weeks of intelligence indicating that BK traveled in a single vehicle, this was supposed to be a very short ambush indeed—one rocket explosion doing the job, with a machine-gun, sniper, and two assault rifles raking the debris just to be sure. Then it would be a speedy exfil for the team, who would vanish before anyone else arrived. And when they did, the kill zone would appear as little more than another factional dispute in a country where such attacks were a daily occurrence.

But two additional trucks changed everything. Worthy's job would be largely the same: take out the lead vehicle at the geographic chokepoint in the canyon below. But now, the team was severely outgunned. They'd lose the element of surprise the instant he fired his rocket, and after that...well, the enemy would get a vote.

Worthy asked, "You think this is a good call, or a bad one?"

To his right, Reilly shifted his position, rocking his massive weapon forward on its bipod. A medic by trade, Reilly had a muscled build that made him a natural pick for wielding the team's sole machinegun.

He replied in a boyish voice, "With David calling the shots, definitely a bad idea. But so far he's always come out alive. Against all odds, sure. But alive."

Worthy nodded and cast a glance at the rifle at his side. As soon as his rocket was fired, that rifle would be his only weapon. He adjusted its position a final time, then stopped moving abruptly.

"You hear that?" he asked.

Reilly glanced right, picking up on the same sound—a vehicle engine churning its way across the winding road below.

There was just one problem: it was coming from the wrong direction.

Reilly pushed himself up on his hands to get a better look, then dropped back down and transmitted.

"Doc has visual on one vehicle inbound from the east. Looks like a civilian sedan."

David replied, "*Is it going to be a problem?*"

"Don't think so. Should pass by a couple minutes ahead of the convoy."

"*Copy,*" David transmitted, "*we are weapons hold until that sedan is out of the kill zone.*"

"Copy," Reilly answered.

After a moment of silence, David transmitted again.

"*Cancer, we are weapons hold, how copy?*"

Begrudgingly, Cancer responded, "*Yeah, yeah. I got it.*"

Worthy smiled. Cancer didn't have the most polished personality on the team, but when it came time for combat, you wanted him on your side of the fight.

He caught a glimpse of the sedan, a battered white vehicle limping over the rough dirt road below.

To Worthy's unease, the sedan began braking before it rolled to a stop in the worst place imaginable—the chokepoint of two canyon walls, a point so narrow that only one vehicle could pass. It was the exact point that Worthy planned to deliver his first rocket.

"He's stopping," Worthy transmitted. "The sedan has stopped right at my chokepoint."

***

I cursed under my breath.

"Did he see us?" I asked.

"*Negative. Must have engine trouble—he's opening the hood.*"

Beside me, Ian transmitted for everyone to hear, "ETA two minutes."

Cancer responded quickly. "*Perfect. We wanted a chokepoint, now it's guaranteed.*"

"Negative," I replied. "We are weapons hold."

"*If that convoy stops at the chokepoint, the guys in the back will pull security and spot us. Then we're fucked.*"

"We're not getting a civilian killed in the crossfire. If we're compromised, we break contact and exfil."

Cancer made no effort to conceal his irritation. "*Think about this, man. It's gonna be self-defense, and we don't have the manpower to fight them off.*"

"We're weapons hold. That's final."

I released the radio switch, a sense of foreboding takin

hold in my gut. As was too often the case in combat, there were no good options—anything you did or failed to do could pair with some absurdity of chance in the ensuing chaos, and turn out to be either your destruction or your salvation.

To my eternal relief, Reilly transmitted, "*Sedan driver has closed his hood and is continuing movement. Clear of the kill zone.*"

Ian followed this up with, "One minute out."

Keying my radio, I spoke quickly.

"Copy all—ambush is a go. We are weapons hot; Racegun, you have control to initiate."

Worthy and Cancer confirmed the order, and I nodded to Ian. "Let's go."

Grabbing our rifles, we high-crawled over the exposed rock to take up firing positions on the dirt road below.

The kill zone was selected for its location between curves—thus ensuring the slowest possible rate of travel—and for the chokepoint in the canyon walls, where any coherent defense from an elevated attack would be difficult if not impossible.

Drawing the rifle stock against my shoulder, I leveled my aim toward the kill zone and listened to the rumble of the approaching convoy. I whispered to Ian, "You good?"

"Yeah." He sounded assured, though what he actually felt in that moment, I had no idea. Ian's specialty was intelligence, not gunslinging, and while I was glad to have him around when his electronic gadgets were required, in the back of my mind he was a tactical liability.

I dismissed the thought as the first pickup came into view, bearing black Islamic State flags. Half a dozen armed men sat in the back. The second truck was just barely visible as the first approached the chokepoint, and with a sense of dread I heard the men begin shouting to each other.

Someone had seen something, and the men were struggling to hoist their weapons upward when I heard a loud explosion—Worthy's rocket firing from the high ground to my right.

I opened fire on the center vehicle, trying to hit the driver through the roof. My gunfire was dwarfed by Reilly's machinegun unleashing a rapid staccato burst, punctuated by the deep booming of Cancer's sniper rifle. Amid the melee, Worthy's rocket found its mark.

The deafening thunderclap of the lead vehicle exploding brought with it an enormous sand cloud that momentarily erased all three trucks from view. I continued pumping rounds into the cloud as fast as I could fire, hearing that all of my teammates were doing the same. In the ideal situation, the lead truck would be immobilized at the chokepoint, but suddenly I saw it bowling forward from the dust and smoke, propelled by the center vehicle now ramming it out of the way.

I desperately adjusted my point of aim to open fire, knowing that my teammates were likewise trying to disable the truck before it could escape. But the canyon road's tight turns resulted in limited sectors of fire, and the lone surviving truck soon careened out of sight.

"Ian," I shouted, "what do we got?"

He was already consulting his tablet to see if the signal from our target's cell phone was stationary or, better yet, destroyed completely. After a few moments, his eyes met mine.

"It's on the move—BK made it out."

I keyed my radio.

"Cease fire, cease fire, cease fire." The chatter of assault rifle and machinegun fire went quiet, and I continued, "BK is on the move. Haul ass to our trucks—we're going to interdict him on the road."

***

Cancer ran down the hillside, his footfalls displacing crumbling chunks of shale. He felt ridiculous in his ghillie suit, the sand-colored strips of burlap trapping his body heat while giving the appearance of a highly flammable human bush scrambling downhill.

Then there was his sniper rifle, which had been fantastic for destroying the rear vehicle's engine block before Worthy's rocket turned the kill zone into a whitewash of smoke and sand. Now, the Barrett .50 cal in his grasp was little more than a five-foot-long, thirty-pound burden threatening to topple him over as he ran toward his team's two vehicles at the bottom of the hill.

Once they'd gotten into position for the ambush, those vehicles were to serve one, and only one, purpose: to speed the men to their pickup point along the Agency ratline, where they'd be whisked out of the country before any coherent search effort could mobilize to find them.

There was nothing in the mission description about tear-assing around Syria, however briefly, in the hunt for an escaped vehicle with their target inside. Still, he could see the logic—there was an overland route by which they could intercept the curving canyon road as it emerged onto flat ground, and perhaps a brief diversion was in order to make it there. If the team arrived quickly enough, they could smoke the target vehicle in a hasty ambush.

The question was whether they could make it there before their target slipped away for good.

Nearing the bottom of the hill, Cancer caught sight of one of his team vehicles ripping east across the desert. Not until he'd threaded his way between boulders at the base of the hill did he see the second—a sand-covered SUV idling with Ian at the wheel.

Cancer yanked the rear door open, angling his massive sniper rifle inside without banging the scope out of alignment. He'd barely felt the seat beneath him before Ian floored the gas, causing the door to slam shut as they gained speed over the desert.

David turned around in the passenger seat and fixed Cancer with an accusatory glare. "What took you so long?"

***

Reilly braced himself in the pickup bed, doing his best to remain standing.

Trying to hold his machinegun stationary on the roof of the cab was like trying to use chopsticks while riding a rodeo bull. The truck pitched and bounced over the rolling terrain, causing the machinegun bipod to carve across the roof in ear-piercing metallic screeches as Reilly fought to stay upright, much less keep the big gun pointed forward.

The ammo presented an additional complication—for the ambush, Reilly had been able to neatly S-fold his ammunition belt in advance. Now, he had to control an ammo bag while keeping the belt angled evenly into the gun, all while trying not to die as Worthy sped them forward.

Ian transmitted, *"Looks like BK is exiting the canyon—we should have eyes-on any second now."*

Reilly scanned the foothills to their front, catching sight of the target vehicle as it emerged a moment later. It was already speeding out of the canyon, perhaps three hundred meters distant and gaining ground fast on the mostly level dirt road. He couldn't tell at a glance if any men—any living men, at least—were in the back, but the pickup itself looked like it had just driven smoking out of some fresh hell. Its front half was coated in black ash and marked by shattered windows; its Islamic State flags flapped in tatters.

Astonishingly, there were survivors in the truck bed—Reilly knew this from the sparking muzzle flashes opening fire toward him.

Grabbing one leg of the bipod to steady it on the roof of the cab, Reilly took aim and loosed a long burst at the truck.

The orange streaks of his tracer rounds interspersed with ball ammunition arced toward the pickup, his first burst landing short as Reilly struggled to adjust his fire. By the third burst he was dropping rounds with general accuracy, the bullets kicking up clouds of sand around the pickup and sparking off the cab as enemy fire continued. Between machinegun bursts, Reilly registered the crack of incoming bullets slicing through the air overhead.

Worthy cut a hard right as they met the dirt road, causing Reilly to nearly fly out of the truck bed.

He slammed a fist on the roof of the cab. "Easy, will you? Trying to shoot here!"

"Sorry about that," Worthy yelled back.

Now, at least, Reilly had a straightforward shot to the target vehicle, which had black smoke billowing in its wake as it struggled to maintain speed. Lining up his iron sights on the fleeing truck, Reilly prepared to fire his next burst– then halted abruptly with two muttered words.

"Well, shit."

Civilian vehicles were pulling off the road, scrambling out of the way to make room for the war-ravaged pickup bowling toward them. It was as if a convoy of innocent bystanders had suddenly appeared at the most inopportune time, and a split second later, Reilly realized why: they were approaching a village, the flat roofs carving a swatch out of the morning horizon.

No matter how well he attempted to aim from the moving vehicle, he could no longer shoot without indiscriminately sending bullets into the civilian populace. He held his fire, fearing that his target was about to escape for good.

But then he saw that it may not matter anyway—the target vehicle was starting to fishtail across the road, the damage to it finally taking hold. As it careened into the outskirts of the village, the rear end pivoted violently to the left. The enemy driver tried to steer out of the turn, but overcorrected and sent his truck into a barreling roll.

**

Flooring the accelerator, Worthy watched the enemy pickup flip sideways three times before crashing to a halt in the village.

He pulled on his seatbelt and shouted to Reilly.

"Hold onto something, bud, I'm going to ram 'em."

Reilly screamed an exasperated response over the roaring engine.

"Well that's just *super*!"

Worthy smiled to himself, thinking that Reilly would do the same if he were behind the wheel. Their jobs had all the potential for physical injury that professional football players faced—minus, of course, the paycheck and fame and cheerleaders. Add in the threat of imminent death at any moment, however, and the two careers were virtually indistinguishable.

He transmitted to the other truck, referring to David by his callsign.

"Suicide, what's your ETA?"

No response.

Could have been a simple radio issue, or could have been David's truck getting tangled up with some enemy force along the way, but in any case, there was no time to consider it.

He was closing with the enemy truck, now inverted on the main road leading into the village. Worthy couldn't tell if there were any survivors, though he made out a few black-clad bodies of ISIS fighters strewn across the dirt.

With the enemy truck's engine block serving as its center of gravity, striking the rear quarter panel should cause the truck to spin and shake up any survivors in the cab. All Worthy needed was a few seconds to dismount and light up his target in the passenger seat, gaining his team a confirmed "jackpot" and getting the hell out of Dodge before enemy reinforcements could arrive.

He was seconds away from impact, barreling into the village at fifty miles per hour, when one of the enemy fighters on the ground recovered his weapon. Worthy scarcely registered the movement, hearing instead the long burst from an AK-47 as bullets pockmarked his windshield and rattled into the engine block.

Worthy cut the steering wheel to the right, keeping his head low as the gunfire continued, growing in volume until his truck ran over the enemy fighter with a lurching *thump*. Then he steered left, aligning his bumper with the enemy truck's rear quarter panel and smashing into it. The impact threw him forward against his seatbelt.

Braking to a sudden stop that brought with it a crashing sound from the truck bed—Reilly and his machinegun coming safely to rest, he presumed—Worthy glanced in his side-view mirror to see the enemy pickup completing a full rotation on its roof. He found his rifle half-wedged in the passenger seat footwell and snatched it up before shouldering his door open.

Worthy absorbed the chaos all around him: women screaming, civilians running for cover, the choking stench of gasoline and smoke from both his own wounded truck and the upended pickup.

He didn't bother checking on his teammate—Reilly could fend for himself, and the best thing Worthy could do for him now was to punch BK's ticket for good, allowing the entire team to escape with mission success intact. Now that they were compromised, every passing second in the Syrian village increased the danger to their lives. With David calling the shots, that danger wasn't likely to end until BK was dead.

Worthy raced to close the distance to the enemy vehicle, skidding to a halt beside the engine block before kneeling to take aim within the cab. Gunfire had carved long scrapes along the cab before ricocheting or boring into the truck, whose windshield was shattered by the triple roll that had crippled it for good.

But the truck was empty.

Before Worthy could fully process the implications of this discovery, he heard Reilly's belt of machinegun ammo jangling as his teammate ran toward him.

"I'm fine, in case you were wondering."

Worthy rose to a crouch, scanning the surrounding buildings in a desperate attempt to determine BK's location. They would have to get off the street in a matter of seconds—he and Reilly were completely exposed to view from countless buildings, any one of which could hold enemy combatants ready to deal themselves into a gunfight.

Just as this thought occurred to him, sparking muzzle flashes erupted from a darkened window across the street, and the first bullets impacted the truck to his front.

***

Ian sped toward the village, catching his first glimpse of Worthy and Reilly: they were pinned down behind the wreckage of the enemy truck, rounds kicking up sand around them. He couldn't tell where the enemy fire was coming from, but apparently the men in his truck could.

From the passenger seat, David asked, "Cancer, where do you want to set up?"

"Park next to that gray building."

Ian squinted through the windshield. Half the buildings in the village were gray. He steered toward the nearest one on the left.

"Not *that* gray building," Cancer reprimanded him, "the one to the right! How am I supposed to engage from over there?"

Ian adjusted course, suddenly far out of his depth. These

men were all seasoned fighters; by contrast, he was an intelligence operative, more suited to analysis than combat. Sure, he could shoot and move when he had to, but he lacked his teammates' reptilian reflexes. If he could have somehow manned his surveillance equipment from a remote location, he knew that David would have kept him off the firing line.

He slowed as they approached the building, and Cancer spoke again.

"Park with the bumper facing our two o'clock."

Ian cut the wheel and braked to a halt, expecting some shouted order or criticism, but instead, David said calmly, "Ian, on me."

That was it, he thought; three words, no further explanation of where they were going or why.

Then the two men were out of the vehicle, David circling behind it and Cancer setting the bipod of his sniper rifle on the hood.

Ian was prepared to run straight toward the row of buildings opposite the enemy truck, and instead saw David cut left and begin a semicircle route.

Ian stutter-stepped and changed course to follow, hearing Cancer's voice over his earpiece.

"*Get outta the way, asshole.*"

He suddenly realized David's circuitous route was to clear a line of fire for Cancer, and he'd barely made it four steps when the sniper rifle blasted behind him.

It was a monumental sound, a .50 caliber gunshot heard at close range that was followed by several more at two-second intervals. Ian saw gaping holes being bored below the window of a building directly ahead of him. That was exactly where David was heading.

Guess that's where the bad guys are, Ian thought. David never moved this quickly unless there was some risk of death to be taunted.

Ian struggled to keep up, bursting through the doorway and moving to the corner opposite David. He visually cleared one corner, then the next, coming to a halt in preparation for David's announcement that the room was clear.

But David was already moving into the next room, not knowing or caring that Ian could barely keep pace.

Apparently Cancer had seen them enter, because his voice crackled over Ian's earpiece.

"*Shifting fire.*"

By now Ian was in the next room, trying to clear his corners but instead cracking his knee against a side table that crashed into a couch. Then Worthy transmitted, "*Racegun and Doc consolidating on target building.*"

"*Copy,*" David replied. Ian only heard the response over his earpiece, not in person—David had already moved into the next room. Ian rushed to follow, entering a kitchen with an open door leading into an alley.

David stood beside the doorway, his barrel angled outside. Ian started to move to him, then noted with surprise that two young women were in the room, both tucked into the corner.

Ian raced to David's back, giving his shoulder a squeeze to indicate he was ready to move.

But instead of flowing outside to continue the hunt for BK, David kept his eyes forward and asked, "They here yet?"

Ian blinked. "Who?"

As if on cue, Worthy and Reilly charged into the room.

They'd just been pinned down and very nearly shot, yet both men looked calmer than Ian felt in that moment. Worthy gently pushed Ian out of the way, assuming the number two position behind David. "My truck's down, engine is shot out," he said quietly.

Reilly nodded to the two women and said, "Hello, ladies," before jostling into the number three position, relegating Ian to the rear of the stack and muttering, "Pick up rear security."

Then David flowed into the alley, with his team following behind.

**

I moved quickly, scanning for any indication of BK's path. It was impossible to discern his footprints from the countless marks on the dirt path, and I threaded my way around clotheslines and children's bicycles that had been abandoned after shooting had begun.

There wouldn't be much to see—a door left ajar, if I was lucky—but I continued with the grim determination that this was our last opportunity, and the clock was ticking down to BK escaping forever.

Granted, the wheels had already come off this mission. But if we were going to get BK, now was our chance. He was on the run with at least one additional fighter—probably his driver—after Cancer's .50 caliber rounds had sufficiently dissuaded them from remaining in place. We had a very momentary advantage in numbers and firepower, but it wouldn't last. BK's trip hadn't been a social call; he was on his way to meet with some very bad people, who would be arriving any moment to rescue him.

The alley took a sharp turn, paralleling the village's main road. Cancer would have just lost his line of sight to our progress, and I suppose it didn't matter much—any fighting at this point was going to occur up close and personal.

Turning the corner with my rifle raised, I took aim at a figure tucked into the corner junction of two walls—an unarmed man, looking at me not with defiance but eager opportunity. He urgently pointed to the door of the building beside him, and I gave him a nod of understanding before running toward it.

The man didn't know who we were, only that we weren't ISIS, and that seemed to be motivation enough for him to help.

I threw the door open and flowed inside, cutting left to clear a blind corner and hearing my teammates' footsteps spilling inside the building behind me. We began clearing the ground floor, splitting into two-man elements. Worthy and Ian moved into a doorway, and I gave Reilly a moment to sling his heavy machinegun and draw his pistol before I proceeded into the next room.

But it was empty, with only a pair of windows providing a view of the dusty street extending northeast through the village.

And it was through those windows that I saw we were too late.

A convoy of ISIS vehicles was speeding down the main road, black flags waving as fighters jockeyed to take aim from the truck beds. They were two hundred meters distant and closing fast.

I called out, "Reilly, hit them!"

He obliged at once, holstering his pistol and readying his machinegun as I slid a table up the wall beneath the left window. Taking his ammo bag, I waited for him to set his bipod atop the table before linking the short, free-hanging belt of ammunition in his machinegun to the S-folded ammo belt inside the bag.

As soon as I said the word "linked," Reilly opened fire.

His opening salvo decimated the windowpane, with his successive bursts lacing into the convoy's lead vehicle.

The trucks screeched to a halt, the second and third vehicles flanking the first as men scrambled out to return fire. Our radio earpieces had a decibel cutoff to serve as hearing protection, but the tremendous blasts of the machinegun cycling inside a confined space were jaw-rattling nonetheless.

Reilly took hold of the ammo belt with one hand, continuing to fire in short bursts to conserve his dwindling supply.

I transmitted, "Cavalry has arrived—set up local support by fire to hold them off. Cancer, get the truck ready and stand by for an emergency exfil."

"*Copy*," Cancer replied.

Moving to the opposite window, I assessed the situation. My first glimpse told me everything I needed to know: the enemy fighters weren't the most highly trained opponents, but with their numerical advantage, that didn't matter much.

There were five trucks that I could see, and the ISIS fighters were firing indiscriminately into the village. They didn't know exactly where we were, not advancing and not needing to. They weren't coming for us, not yet. They were instead laying down a wall of lead to allow BK to make his way to them.

I took aim and found my first target, a rifleman shooting from behind an open truck door. Before I could squeeze off my first shots, a trio of rounds stitched across his collarbone and face. Judging by the accuracy, Worthy had just wiped him off the battlefield.

Swinging my rifle to the right, I fired four bullets at another fighter, tagging him with at least one round that caused him to drop out of sight. I aimed at the next visible ISIS combatant, who was standing in the open and paid for it with two bullets to the chest.

There was little we could do now but hold our positions and keep the enemy at bay until Cancer was ready to speed us to safety. Maybe—if we were lucky—we could get a clean shot at BK as he made his way to the trucks.

A shrill scream outside the window cut my thoughts short, and I adjusted my position to locate the source.

She was a girl of eight or nine, now crouched behind the insubstantial cover provided by a pile of mud bricks on the opposite side of the street, remnants of some half-remembered repair project that had probably been abandoned at the start of the civil war.

Now the bullets were kicking up sand around her, impacting the bricks to her front and the wall to her side. It was a matter of time before she got struck by a direct hit or a ricochet.

The sight of her seemed to suck all the oxygen from my surroundings; whether I liked it or not, the tactical situation faded completely from my mind. Here was a girl not much older than my own daughter, and I'd placed her in danger. If I didn't do something fast, she'd die because of me.

I was moving for the door before I consciously realized what I was doing, priming for the fastest run of my life. The morning sunshine beyond the doorway was dim behind the sandy clouds kicked up by bullet impacts, and with a final breath, I charged into the open.

There is a certain surreal quality imparted by racing through a hail of enemy gunfire. As my legs pumped in an adrenaline-fueled sprint, my peripheral vision registered the bullet impacts on the dirt road, on the brick and cinder block buildings around me.

The little girl watched my approach, screaming words I couldn't register above the noise and sobbing with terror. I heard the sharp paper-tearing sounds of bullets passing by, released my rifle with one hand, and fell backward into a baseball slide for the remaining few feet between us.

Skidding to a stop on my back, I wrapped my open arm around her chest, hoisted her tight against my side, and rose to a crouch.

The remaining distance to the nearest building corner was only four meters or so, but the few footfalls it took me to get there seemed to take an eternity. I darted for the corner and a narrow alleyway beyond it; the last thing I saw before reaching it was a bullet strike the tan wall, an impact that fired a spray of sand and debris into my eyes.

Then my vision was gone, eyes stinging as I proceeded into the alley by memory alone. I threw my back against the wall, hearing the staccato pops of gunfire continuing beside me. The girl was safe now. I tried to set her down, but it was no use—she clung to my side with animal ferocity, refusing to let go.

I wiped the back of my hand across my eyes until I could make out the foggy, unfocused expanse of alley before me, then found the nearest door and kicked it open.

She was still sobbing as I carried her inside to safety, perhaps uncertain whether she'd been rescued or kidnapped, and in the war-torn hellhole this nation had become, I couldn't blame her.

"It's okay," I said, aiming for a reassuring tone only to be met with a sense of sheer absurdity. There were no good guys or bad guys in this fight, and regardless of our intention—or the greater evils BK could inflict upon civilian masses if left unchecked—we'd nonetheless brought danger into this village, into her home. If I was looking for gratitude, I wasn't going to get it from her.

I tried to set her down again, to get back into the fight unencumbered. But she continued clinging to me with savage intensity, apparently deciding that in this moment I represented the lesser of two evils. I couldn't blame her for that assumption, and struggled to the nearest window to appraise the situation.

The convoy hadn't moved, though the fighters had dispersed to the surrounding structures to hold their line. I scanned the buildings across the street, trying to determine whether the fighters had begun advancing on us, when I caught a sudden flash of movement. I was prepared to duck behind the wall—with the girl clinging to my side, I wasn't about to get the jump on any determined enemy.

But something stopped me from hiding completely. It was a sense of disbelief, the jarring thought that I couldn't possibly be seeing what I was seeing.

I only observed him for a second, a momentary alignment of

angles that caused me to catch a glimpse of the man's face in the window across the street.

For a fleeting moment, we locked eyes—here was my target, the man I'd been sent to kill. We referred to him as BK, but his real name was Bari Khan, and the face that met mine was not Arab but Chinese. A Uyghur dissident, he'd found not-so-strange bedfellows in ISIS, with many of the same goals and enemies.

Bari Khan's face was covered in dust and glistening blood.

But his eyes were strangely unemotional, coolly in control. He seemed to be appraising me with disinterest, making no attempt to take aim.

I wasn't about to return the favor. Maneuvering my rifle around the girl, I struggled to bring my sights to bear on him.

It was too late. He was gone.

That was it, I knew at once. My team was stretched too thin to pursue any further—had, in fact, been stretched too thin to begin pursuing after the ambush failed to kill him. Our survival streak would end if we pushed our luck any further.

Moments later, the incoming gunfire abated almost completely as a group of enemy trucks whipped wild U-turns in the street, accelerating out of the village as my team continued firing at them. Two trucks remained abandoned, their engine blocks shot out by Reilly's machinegun.

Bari Khan was gone, this time for good, and his departure spelled something worse for our team. ISIS wasn't going to let our presence remain uncontested, and regardless of where they were taking the terrorist leader we'd been sent to kill, I knew at once that a larger opposition force was on its way to kill us.

I transmitted, "Cancer, they're gone. Need you to bring up the truck ASAP to get us out of here. Come up the main road until you see us."

He responded with one word: "*Moving.*"

Before I could attempt to pry the little girl off my side, Reilly transmitted, "*Suicide, you need support?*"

"Negative. Just flag down Cancer and I'll meet you at the truck."

Then I heard running footsteps approaching and immediately regretted my declaration to move alone. Whoever was coming toward me was doing so in a hurry, and it was too late to request help without him hearing me—and with confrontation imminent and the little girl still clinging to me like a spider monkey, my only advantage was the element of surprise.

I darted to the corner beside the doorway and knelt to keep the girl tucked behind my body. Then I aimed my rifle.

A man burst into the room so quickly that I almost fired out of blind reaction. His hands were empty, shirt taut against his torso, leaving no room for a suicide vest. This was no enemy fighter, but a panic-stricken man with tears staining his face.

Her father.

The man's eyes were wide, uncomprehending of the terror around him. He'd probably struggled to survive amid the endless bloodshed of the Syrian Civil War, only to find a group of armed men doing battle at his doorstep through no fault of his own.

He was just trying to safeguard his family the best he could, the same as I would have in his situation. The difference between us was little more than our place of birth.

I lowered my rifle and stood to hand him the child. She immediately clung to him, and as the man's eyes met mine with impossible gratitude, I gave him a silent nod—Arabic wasn't my specialty.

To my surprise, he addressed me in English.

"Thank you."

I felt a goofy half-grin spread across my face as the dim euphoria of recognition set in—if I'd been born elsewhere, this could just as easily have been my own daughter being saved. Then, I gave the only response I could think to muster.

"You're welcome."

I only had a moment to study his long, thin face and well-trimmed beard. Then he turned, keeping his daughter in his grasp as he moved not outside but rather up the stairs to the second floor. I realized in that moment that this wasn't some random structure I'd been occupying, but the girl's home.

Their departure jarred me to reality—my team was compromised in Syria, and the enemy surely didn't intend on letting us leave if they could prevent it.

The sound of an engine approached outside, and I knew Cancer was almost at my position. Then all hell broke loose as an automatic weapon began firing in wild bursts from just up the street.

I looked outside to find the source, and saw that the only possible location was from behind a partially finished cinder block wall jutting out from a building. Whoever this remaining enemy was, he was blasting rounds in our direction, shooting up the sides of buildings and shattering windows.

I transmitted, "Doc, can you drop that wall?"

"*Negative, I'm black on ammo.*"

"Anyone else got a shot?"

Worthy answered, "*No, we can't see him from here.*"

The remaining fighter was firing wildly while screaming in Arabic. He'd either not heard the order to withdraw, decided to ignore it, or had been sent to cover BK's withdrawal. The circumstances mattered precious little to us at present—he was shooting at us, and we couldn't flee the scene until he was dealt with. A single errant bullet at this point could disable our lone remaining truck, and I didn't want to test our odds with a commandeered local vehicle.

I also didn't want to take the time to maneuver forward until we could get a clear shot—not when there was a much quicker option available.

"Cancer," I transmitted, "we need you to get him. We'll cover you. He's behind the cinder block wall to your front."

He didn't respond; instead, I saw his tan SUV roll to a stop at the side of the road before he got out, hoisting his heavy sniper rifle and shaking his head in irritation. He marched angrily toward the cinder block wall, where the single entrenched fighter was still firing upward. Cancer's massive sniper rifle was intended for mile-long shots, not working up close and personal; but in the current situation, it was the best tool for the job.

Cancer moved along the wall, following the sound of gunfire on the other side. When he came abreast of the noise, he stopped, knelt, and strained to lift the enormous Barrett until its muzzle was level with the cinder block surface.

Then he fired a single shot, a deafening *boom* whose blast sent an enormous cloud of sand dust washing over him. The bullet ejected a spray of concrete out of the other side of the wall, bowling the enemy fighter over in a whirling froth of blood and bone fragments that painted the ground red.

I transmitted, "You got him."

Cancer's voice shot back over my earpiece.

"*No shit.*"

I shrugged and keyed my radio again.

"Consolidate on the truck. Let's get out of here while we can."

I ran toward the SUV, now idling with Ian at the wheel. Sliding onto the passenger seat, I turned to my team as Ian wheeled around and accelerated out of the village.

Worthy had piled into the storage space in the back of the SUV, and Reilly and Cancer fought to maneuver their giant weapons in the backseat. Combat always looked so cool in the movies, but the current dogpile reflected the reality we'd all experienced before: real war was an unglamorous, messy process of improvisation, and it would either claim your life or leave scars both physical and psychological.

I transmitted over my command frequency, "Paradise Seven One, this is Suicide Actual."

"Send your traffic."

"We are no-joy. Require emergency exfiltration, time now."

Long seconds elapsed before the response, the pause serving as an audible reminder of the collective disappointment from our mission failure.

"Copy, assets are standing by at the link-up point."

I moved my hand away from the radio switch, suddenly feeling like I'd run the hundred-yard dash while holding my breath. As soon as the adrenaline of battle faded, the body prioritized everything denied to it during the fight: water, oxygen, rest.

Ian looked over at me from the driver's seat.

"David, you think we'll ever get another shot at this guy?"

I adjusted the rifle between my legs, barrel pointed down to the floor.

Swallowing against a dry throat, I replied, "I don't know."

It was a good question, of course—the CIA had sent us after Bari Khan for a reason, and now he was on the loose with the full knowledge that he'd been located by men who were trying to kill him. He was about to go into hiding, and there was no telling if he'd surface again before an untold number of civilians paid the ultimate price.

But I knew one thing for certain: if the Agency succeeded in locating Bari Khan again, then my team sure as hell wasn't going to fail a second time.

* * *

Get your copy today at
severnriverbooks.com/series/shadow-strike-series

ALSO BY JASON KASPER

American Mercenary Series
Greatest Enemy
Offer of Revenge
Dark Redemption
Vengeance Calling
The Suicide Cartel
Terminal Objective

Shadow Strike Series
The Enemies of My Country
Last Target Standing
Covert Kill
Narco Assassins
Beast Three Six

Spider Heist Thrillers
The Spider Heist
The Sky Thieves
The Manhattan Job
The Fifth Bandit

Standalone Thriller
Her Dark Silence

To find out more about Jason Kasper and his books, visit
severnriverbooks.com/authors/jason-kasper

ABOUT THE AUTHOR

Jason Kasper is the USA Today bestselling author of the Spider Heist, American Mercenary, and Shadow Strike thriller series. Before his writing career he served in the US Army, beginning as a Ranger private and ending as a Green Beret captain. Jason is a West Point graduate and a veteran of the Afghanistan and Iraq wars, and was an avid ultramarathon runner, skydiver, and BASE jumper, all of which inspire his fiction.

Sign up for Jason Kasper's reader list at
severnriverbooks.com/authors/jason-kasper

jasonkasper@severnriverbooks.com

Printed in the United States
by Baker & Taylor Publisher Services